Orysia Dawydiak

Rika's Shepherd

FROM HACKMATACK-NOMINATED AUTHOR

Orysia Dawydiak

Rika's Shepherd

The Acorn Press
Charlottetown
2018

Text © 2018 by Orysia Dawydiak

ACORNPRESS

P.O. Box 22024
Charlottetown, Prince Edward Island
C1A 9J2
acornpresscanada.com

Edited by Penelope Jackson
Copy edited by Laurie Brinklow
Designed by Matt Reid
Printed in Canada

Library and Archives Canada Cataloguing in Publication

Dawydiak, Orysia, 1952-, author
Rika's shepherd / Orysia Dawydiak.

Issued in print and electronic formats.
ISBN 978-1-77366-001-1 (softcover).--ISBN 978-1-77366-002-8
(HTML)

I. Title.

PS8607.A968R55 2018   jC813'.6   C2018-901119-X
                                               C2018-901120-3

Canada Council   Conseil des Arts
for the Arts   du Canada

The publisher acknowledges the support of the Government
of Canada through the Canada Book Fund of the Department
of Canadian Heritage for our publishing activities. We also
acknowledge the support of the Canada Council for the
Arts for our publishing program.

For my dear friend, Marsha Peterson,
whose dedication to the animals and people
in her life has amazed and inspired me,
and made me a better person.

Chapter One

Rika pulled on her denim overalls and looked down towards her feet. The knees were nearly worn out, and the hems ended well above her slender ankles. She could ask for a new pair, but she'd had these overalls less than a year, and she loved the Border Collie embroidered on the pocket. In the last few months, Rika had gone through a major growth spurt and was now the tallest girl in her class at school, taller even than most of the boys. Her mother would have patched the knees and taken the hems down, but Rika never cared for sewing or mending clothes.

She stepped into her rubber boots, tucked in the pant legs, and headed for the barn. The sound of bawling cattle could be heard well before she opened the door.

"Papa? Do you need help here?" she called through the din. At the far end of the barn, she could see the blond head of her father as he moved calmly amongst the cows, securing each one into her individual milking stall.

"No, Rika," he shouted over the jostling cattle. "Go tend to your sheep. When I brought in the cows, I noticed they were gathered at one end of the field."

Rika loved her little flock of sheep. Most of her school friends couldn't understand her attachment to them, even though many of them lived on farms like she did. The horsey crowd with their expensive outfits and fine leather saddles and tack were often contemptuous of kids whose families raised beef, pigs, and crops. Although she helped her father manage their dairy herd, the sheep belonged to her alone.

It was her mother, Ingrid, who had first suggested that perhaps Rika might enjoy tending them, as Ingrid had when she was a girl on the family farm in Holland. Nearly six years ago, Rika's parents bought the first two ewes for her ninth birthday, and now she owned one of the best horned Dorset flocks on Prince Edward Island. After her mother died, her father, Willem, suggested they change their farm name from *van Wijk's Holsteins* to *Willemrika Farm*, since they had expanded to include sheep. When Rika was ten, her father made her an official business partner and put her in charge of the sheep. She took on the new role with wholehearted enthusiasm at a time when they were still grappling with grief.

What gave Rika the greatest joy was to look out over the pastures where her sheep grazed and watch lambs cavort around their mothers. One at a time, they would bounce straight up into the air like corn popping in a hot pan, then land and tear off all together in a manic dash to no destination in particular. All the while, their mothers continued to graze, unconcerned. Within moments the lambs would be back and under their dams, punching the udders with their heads to coax down the milk they needed to fuel their next round of games.

Her father's comment about the flock concerned Rika. She wheeled around and ran down a path through a thicket of trees, her fine, unruly hair flying behind her like a ragged golden flag. She heard nothing out of the ordinary as she approached the east pasture with its flock of fifteen ewes and their many lambs. Even so, from a distance Rika could sense that her sheep were upset. The flock was more tightly bunched than usual and they were not grazing.

She slowed to a walk, not wanting to startle them, but they had already spotted her: their wary heads were up and their ears pricked forward. Two or three began to bleat when they recognized her. She stopped at the gate and swept her eyes over the flock and the surrounding pasture edged with bushes and trees. At this time of the evening, the lambs were normally racing and leaping in wild circles, not huddled near their mothers as they were now.

When Rika finally opened the gate to walk through, the flock broke up and rushed around her, anticipating treats. No matter how stressed they might be, her sheep were always willing to eat grain. "Silly sheep, stop moving around so I can count you. Twenty-four, twenty-five, twenty-six..." Lambs were missing.

"Sheep, sheep, sheep!" she called in a high voice. No answer from the wayward lambs. Rika's heart felt like it would burst through her chest. Where were they? She pushed through the flock, the sheep bleating their displeasure, and made her way toward the thick hedgerow at the edge of the pasture. As she neared the tree line she noticed slight movements on the ground. Had something, some animal, perhaps, gotten through the fence? Impossible. The six-strand electric fence was supposed to be impenetrable. Papa said they had the best fencing on PEI, and they had just checked it last week. The line current was high enough to fry hot dogs, he'd said.

Then, as Rika watched in horror, a tan, doglike creature stood up, and another beside it, just fifty feet in front of her. Their muzzles were dark, but even at that distance, even in the dusk, she knew it was blood. Rika sucked in her breath, her jaws clamped shut. The coyotes stared back at her across that space as if waiting for her next move, then finally turned and slowly, deliberately, slipped under the lowest fence wire and retreated into the darkness of the forest.

Rika's knees were about to give way, but she forced herself to move forward. From ten feet she could see enough to know that three of her lambs were dead and partly eaten. She screamed and crumpled onto the ground, clutching her stomach.

"No, no!" she wailed. Tears blurred the horrible sight as she knelt on the cold, hard earth. Rika, still sobbing, was barely aware when arms encircled her shoulders, helped her rise, and gently guided her back to the house.

"But Papa, how could they get through?" Rika cried. She sat up in her bed later that evening, still in shock. "It wasn't supposed to happen! And they told us there weren't any coyotes anywhere near here. They lied!"

"Rika, Rika, we knew there were coyotes on the Island." Willem van Wijk sat at the edge of her bed, stroking the blond head of his distressed daughter. "It was just a matter of time. That is why we put in the electric fence."

"But it didn't work! They got through, didn't they?" she protested. "I don't see why I can't sleep in the barn tonight. The sheep are upset. What if the coyotes come back?"

"The sheep are safe in the barn, Rika. Nothing can get in there. Tomorrow we will talk to the Department of Agriculture and tell them what happened. Perhaps they can give us other suggestions to keep the coyotes out. We might want to consider a guard animal. What do you think?" He patted her hands clutching the bed covers under her chin.

"My lambs are dead." Fresh tears rolled down Rika's pale cheeks. "Nothing will help. They're dead." She withdrew her hands and sank down from the pillow, pulling the covers over her head. Willem could hear her soft sobs through the wool duvet. He sighed and stood up.

"Ya, we will attend to this problem tomorrow. Good night, Rika," he said in his soft Dutch accent and turned off the light.

There was no response from under the covers except for occasional shuddering.

In the five years since Rika's mother had died, they had never lost a single animal on the farm. Although Willem and Rika talked about the cycles of birth and death, she had never cared for endings.

Chapter Two

Rika slept poorly that night and was back in the barn much earlier than usual to check on her flock. The sheep baaed their typical greetings, though she noticed that the ewes who had lost lambs were more restless than the others. Fortunately, each of the three bereaved mothers still had one of her twins remaining.

By the time lambs were three months old, the dams stopped counting their babies and were less likely to notice if one went missing. In fact, the lambs were now old enough to be weaned from their mothers, something Rika planned to do in the next week or two. Ewes and lambs alike called impatiently for the oats she scooped from a bin outside their pen. Once she had filled the feeders with grain, only the sound of shuffling and crunching could be heard. It always amazed her how quickly lambs learned to eat grass and grain—they were often sampling solid food within a week of birth. Now they had the teeth to grind grain and there was enough grass to graze. When the lambs were separated from their mothers, she could cut back on feeding the costly grain to the ewes. They only converted it into milk while the lambs were nursing. Meanwhile, the lambs would still have some access to grain as well as fresh grass as they grew and filled out in a nearby green pasture.

Rika sat on a bale of straw and watched them eat in the dimly lit barn. She shivered in the cold, damp air, recalling fragments of disturbing dreams from the night before. In one scene, she had been a passenger in a car racing down a narrow road that wound past icy, grey, steep-sided hills. In the next instant, she had been standing inside a building in front of a tall door. Her feet had suddenly felt cold and wet, and when she looked down, she saw a red fluid oozing out from under the door. The thick red goo started to fill the room, creeping up her body like liquid nitrogen, freezing her into an immovable block of ice.

Rika remembered waking up at this point, standing beside her bed, shaking and sweaty in the chilly air before she crawled back under the covers. She hadn't had such a bizarre dream in a very long while. Just after her mother's death, the dream had recurred night after night. She used to struggle to stay awake, terrified of sleep and the repeating nightmares. Last night again she lay in bed, wide awake and miserable, remembering what she had seen earlier that evening.

She thought about her dead lambs lying in bloody sacks in a cool room behind the milking parlour and squeezed her eyes tight. Papa told her that he had brought them in so the fish and wildlife people could have a look before he buried them. They would determine if the lambs had been killed by coyotes or stray dogs, he said. What difference did it make? She already knew they were coyotes; she had seen them with her own eyes.

A loud baa brought Rika back to the present. The sheep had finished eating their breakfast ration, so she broke up a bale of hay and tossed it into their manger. They wouldn't be let out on the pasture again until the coyote problem was solved. Anyway, she had enough hay for a few more weeks. She had let them out because grass was growing again and they hated being cooped up in the barn after a long winter. She'd wanted them to be happy, and instead she had become an accessory to murder.

Rika sniffled, her feet dragging as she returned to the house. She dreaded the thought of going to school that day. "Papa, my stomach aches. Maybe I should stay home," she said, scowling at the toast on her plate.

"You know you get cramps when you are anxious," Willem said as he poured her a glass of milk.

Rika managed to swallow two bites of toast and drink half the milk before she pushed away from the table. She shouldered her backpack and trudged to the bus stop at the end of their long driveway. While she waited, she kicked at small chunks of red dirt by the side of the road. Papa didn't understand. She would have to tell Liz what had happened the evening before, but what if she burst into tears? That would be horrible, everyone gawking at her, thinking how silly she was. Or worse, feeling sorry for her.

Her best friend was already on the bus when Rika climbed aboard. Short and sturdy, with a mass of brown, curly hair, Liz was the fourth in a farm family of eight children and was always in good humour.

"Hey, Rika, you don't look so good. What's wrong?" Liz asked when Rika took a seat next to her.

Rika clutched her hands together and looked away. She swallowed, then stared hard at the back of the seat in front of her for a few seconds before she could speak. "Coyotes killed three of my lambs yesterday!" she blurted out. Liz gasped, and several heads turned toward them. Rika had not meant to speak so loudly.

"Coyotes?" someone asked.

"How big were they?" someone else shouted.

"How many? Did you see them?" Billy Miller wanted to know.

Rika's face reddened at the barrage of questions. Liz

gripped her arm in sympathy while Rika recounted in detail what had happened. By the time they reached school, the entire bus was buzzing with comments and more questions. The last time coyotes had attacked in the area, they had taken Billy's terrier, or so he claimed. Before that, it was a newborn calf in Bart Buell's back field. No one had actually seen the coyotes take the dog or kill the calf, but the owners swore they had heard that distinctive yipping and howling close by on the night of each incident.

Rika sensed the sympathy and awe around her that she had actually witnessed the killers herself. For a moment in the spotlight, she felt like someone who had accomplished an amazing feat—then she was consumed with guilt.

Later that day during her free period, Rika slipped into the computer room to send an email to her cousin Elly in Holland. Although she had just written a letter to Elly that weekend, she couldn't wait to tell her about the coyote attack. They had a computer at home for the farm business, but Rika could only use it to write up school assignments or letters to print—she was not allowed email or Internet at home. This was a sore point with her; she hated the looks on her friends' faces when they asked for her email address and she had to explain that she couldn't receive their messages at home. They'd have to telephone her instead, the old-fashioned way. She did not want anyone to feel sorry for her because her father was so strict and she had no mother. Most of her friends didn't understand that she actually enjoyed helping Papa with the farm and being in charge of her own flock of sheep.

Her cousin Elly didn't understand either, though she lived on a dairy farm herself. Elly, who was two years older than Rika, attended a big city high school and had very different interests and tastes. Still, Rika had always looked up to her cousin, especially after her mother died. Elly became someone she relied on, who took the time to write and comfort her, like an older sister who understood Rika's loss and loneliness, even though they'd only met in person three times, once being at her mother's funeral and most recently on a trip to Holland three years later.

Now Elly's occasional letters and emails described her latest boyfriend, the coolest fashions, hairstyles, and rock bands. Rika envied her cousin's freedom and outgoing nature. She herself felt awkward around most boys, except for the few who lived on farms nearby—boys she'd known since childhood. Still, she complained to Elly about Willem's tight reins so her cousin didn't think she was too backward or unpopular. She also wrote how she desperately wanted a Border Collie to train to herd her sheep, and that she wished their cranky old veterinarian would retire soon. The two girls corresponded by letter occasionally, but mostly it was via email, which Rika accessed either from school or from Liz's home. Rika justified keeping this harmless little secret from Papa since he was being so unreasonable.

Monday afternoon seemed to drag on forever. By the end of the day, the whole school had heard about Rika's tragedy. She had a lot of sympathy from everyone, even from students she hardly knew. She could barely say a word when Errol Keir spoke to her—one of the few boys who was taller than Rika, not to mention one of the cutest guys and smartest students in tenth grade. He was not in her homeroom class, so she was surprised he knew her name. The kids on the bus wished her well when she got off at her stop. Rika waved a thank you as the bus pulled away, and ran with new energy up her driveway.

"Papa! I'm home!" she called out, throwing her backpack down on a chair. She listened for his voice, then heard some mumbling from the back. Rika approached the office so she could hear better.

"What is the name again? Ya, uh-huh. Phone number? Good. So, I just call and arrange for a convenient time? I see. Ya. Thank you, Fulton. Good-bye."

Rika heard the phone being slipped back in its base, and poked her head into the room.

"Ah, Rika, hello! How was school today?" Willem stood up from his desk, smiling at his daughter. People who didn't know them might have guessed he was an older brother of Rika's despite their twenty-one-year difference. Both were fair-haired, tall, and slim, and while Willem was often smiling, Rika tended to wear a serious expression.

Rika's thoughts were far from school by this time. "Oh, school, who cares?" When Willem raised his eyebrows, she continued, "It was okay, I guess. Everybody was nice to me when they heard what happened." She paused. "Did you talk to anyone about the coyotes?"

"Ya, I just finished speaking to Fulton Lund, the sheep specialist in the Department of Agriculture, and to someone in the wildlife section. You were right, of course, about the coyotes. They tell us the coyotes are here to stay, but they had some ideas. Fulton said I should call the trapper Blaine Doiron."

"Trapper? Will he kill the coyotes if he catches them?"

"I believe so, Rika. The trap he uses is very effective if he can bait it properly. When he catches a coyote, he will destroy it. I am sure he will be humane; the coyote would not suffer."

Rika's brows were knitted together in concern. "What if a cat or dog comes along? Couldn't they be caught in the trap and hurt?"

"I think the bait he uses will attract only coyotes. Anyway, he will place them far from where cats and dogs are supposed to be."

"But the Stevensons have all those barn cats, and they go

everywhere. And Danny Boy, Mrs. MacIsaac's Malamute sometimes visits. What if they get trapped?"

"Rika, if Mrs. MacIsaac's dog is sniffing around our pastures, he might also hurt your sheep. Anyway, I really do not think he goes that far into the woods. If you like, we will ask Mrs. MacIsaac to keep her dog tied up while the traps are set. Dogs should not be allowed to run free, even in the country. It is a wonder Danny Boy has not been hit by a car yet. Look, Rika, when Blaine comes over, you can ask him all these questions about trapping. How would that be?"

"Okay, I guess." Rika was troubled, but could not argue further. "Did you take out the pork chops for supper?" she asked.

"Ya, Rika, just as you requested." Willem smiled at her as she turned and walked into the kitchen. She had a busy life and little time to dwell on disappointments.

The next Saturday, Rika took her friends Liz and Stirling to the far end of the east pasture. They wanted to see the place where her lambs had met their doom, as Stirling had put it. It was a chilly April day, and rain had been falling on and off all morning. Rika wore her bright blue wool tam, Liz could only manage earmuffs over her thick hair, and Stirling braved the icy winds bareheaded. He was taller than Liz, but a half-inch shorter than Rika. He jogged ahead of the two girls, hoping to see coyotes.

"It was just over there by the trees." Rika pointed to a spot near the fence.

"Are you sure the power was on when the coyotes came through?" Stirling asked.

Rika glowered at him. "Yes, I'm sure. It's always on." She stared into the trees, wondering where the coyotes might be. A strong gust of wind just then caused all three to step backwards and brace themselves.

"Did you hear something out there?" Liz asked, pointing toward the trees. "Like a dog howling?"

Rika and Stirling strained to listen, but all they heard was wind in the trees sounding like waves roaring on a stormy beach.

"Maybe a cat?" Rika suggested. She had heard the noise earlier, but could not identify it.

"Where did Blaine set those traps, Rika?" Stirling asked.

"I'm not exactly sure. Just the other side of the trees, I think. Papa said not to disturb the place, so I haven't looked for them."

"What was that?" Liz jumped backwards. The cry was unmistakable. "That was too creepy. Maybe we should go back."

"What, are you afraid of coyotes? Remember what Syd told us? They don't hunt in packs like wolves, you know. You're not scared, are ya?" he taunted her.

"No, I'm not scared, but—oh God, what was that? You heard it, too!" This time even Rika and Stirling shivered.

"I have a bad feeling about this. What if it's an animal caught in a trap?"

"Wow, wouldn't it be neat if it was a coyote?" Stirling rubbed his hands together, and his freckled face broke into a gleeful smile.

"Stirling, you are so gross. What if it's some poor cat? What then?" Liz glared at him.

Rika twisted her tam so her hair made a tangled halo. "It might be a coyote or a dog, but it sounds like it's hurt. I don't like this."

Stirling threw his hands up in the air and strode toward the fence. "I don't believe you guys. First you freak out about coyotes killing lambs, now you're upset because a coyote might be hurt. Those coyotes deserve to die!" Stirling walked along the fence as though he were searching for something. While the girls looked on in amazement, he found a spot with a hollow and then slipped under the lowest strand of wire. Rika had no idea it was so easy to go under the fence without being shocked. Stirling stood up on the other side with his hands on his hips. "Well, are you coming or not?"

Rika and Liz followed his example, taking great care not to contact the electrified wire. Soon they were prying their way into the thick undergrowth of black spruce, spindly maples, and alder bushes, using their arms to shield their eyes from the sharp branches. Occasionally they stopped and listened for the cries. The noise seemed to move all around them, a ghostly howler who did not wish to be found. Liz grabbed at the back of Rika's jacket whenever she could reach her. What if Syd was wrong about a coyote pack? she thought. What if these were crosses between wolves and coyotes? What if there was a pack of them just waiting in the bushes?

They halted again after not hearing the cries for some time. Inside the woods, the sound of the wind was muffled. A sharp cry very near them startled all three, and Liz shrieked. Stirling jumped off to the right, and Rika whirled around, looking wildly through the branches. Liz stood immobile, hardly breathing.

"Over here!" Stirling shouted. Rika snatched at Liz's arm and pulled her along to where Stirling stood, staring down at the ground.

"Oh my God! Gross!" Liz shuddered and averted her eyes from the sight.

Rika felt her stomach twist at the sight. A small coyote, not fully grown, lay still among the leaves at the base of a birch tree. It panted in shallow, rapid bursts, its pointed mouth wide open, squinting gold eyes alert and vigilant. Rika could see that one hind leg was caught in the trap and protruded from the other end at an unnatural angle. For the second time that week, she felt her knees buckling. Again, she consciously stiffened her body, fighting the urge to scream and run. Her arm reached ahead and she grasped Stirling's jacket.

"Let's go," she commanded. "We have to get some help."

"What?" Stirling resisted. "You want to the help the coyote? You crazy?"

"Look, butthead, that's just a pup. We can't leave him there." Rika's glare broke through Stirling's bravado.

"Yeah, all right, let's go. Blaine will take care of him."

Liz was already on her way, frantically pushing through the brush ahead of them. Rika turned to follow, choking on her frustration and guilt. She couldn't help thinking it was her fault that an innocent coyote pup would die because she had failed to be a good shepherd. Maybe his parents had killed her lambs, but he shouldn't have to pay for it. It wasn't fair. Life just wasn't fair.

Chapter Three

"What happened after you reported the trapped coyote pup?" Syd asked. She sat with Rika and Liz in a corner of the hall where she taught 4-H dog obedience classes. Liz's black-and-white Border Collie, Trixie, lay patiently at their feet, her intense eyes fixed on her owner's face. She thumped her tail whenever Liz spoke.

Syd, whose full name was Sydney Anne Godfrey, was born with a head of thick, wavy red hair, the same colour as that of Prince Edward Island's fictional sweetheart, Anne of Green Gables. That hair had caused her some grief in her youth, so she rarely divulged her middle name. At the age of twenty-nine, Syd's hair colour had become a rich auburn, and she wore it long, usually woven in a French braid that hung halfway down her back. Her freckles and cream complexion matched her hair perfectly. Syd was of average height, strongly built, and she nearly always wore a cheery smile. Warm brown eyes gave her a gentle look, very much in contrast to her aging uncle, Alistair Godfrey, the irascible veterinarian who Rika complained about. Syd, also trained as a veterinarian, had just returned to the Island to start working at her uncle Alistair's clinic.

Syd knew that Rika was hoping to get her own Border Collie as soon as she had saved enough money to buy a good pup from working parents. She was sympathetic when Rika told her about the coyote attack. Then Liz described how they found the trapped coyote.

"So Rika's dad phoned the trapper," Liz continued.

"Blaine Doiron," Rika added.

"He came right over, but Rika's dad wouldn't let us go back there with them. Anyway, I didn't want to see the poor little thing again. It was awful," Liz finished with a pained expression.

"He killed an innocent pup. He killed it!" Rika's voice had risen and her face flushed.

Syd, her expression serious, leaned back in her chair and hooked her thumbs in the pockets of her faded black jeans. "I'm sure this hasn't been easy for you." She looked directly at Rika. "You don't want to see any animals suffer, not your sheep *or* the coyotes, do you?"

"No way!" Rika agreed.

"Me neither!" Liz seconded.

"Rika, have you talked to your dad about using a guard animal? You know, like a guard dog, or a guard donkey?"

Liz giggled. "Guard donkey?"

"Well, my dad mentioned it, but he decided to call the trapper first. Maybe it costs too much." Rika stared down at the ground, tugging at the loose curtain of hair that nearly hid her face. "I think a guard dog would be cool. Aren't they those big white dogs with the weird names? Are there any on the Island?"

Syd smiled at Rika's enthusiasm. "There are both guard donkeys and guard dogs on PEI. I can give you the names of a few people who use them, and a breeder if you're interested."

Rika's face clouded again. "Do guard animals kill coyotes?"

"It's possible, but normally they just chase them away. Once the coyotes learn that these guard animals are on duty, they usually look for food somewhere else. End of problem, for that flock anyway. With a guard dog, you'd need good fencing, though. You have electric fencing, don't you, Rika?"

"Yes," she replied with a sour face, "but the coyotes still got in."

Syd leaned forward again. "So first you need to talk to people who use these animals. Perhaps you should discuss this with your dad before you call them."

"Oh yeah, I'll do that. I wish he'd never called the trapper. I'm not letting that man back on our property!" Rika stamped her foot. Just then the door burst open and a large, panting dog lurched in, dragging his ten-year-old owner behind him.

"Hello, Andrew! Hello, Comet!" Syd greeted the students, then rose from her chair to help the boy untangle himself from his exuberant Golden Retriever. "Rika, remind me to give you those names before you leave class tonight."

Rika could hardly wait to talk to her father, but she settled in to watch the class like she did every week. Only this time, she pictured herself with a large white pup trotting next to her as they circled the room, practising their sits, downs, and heeling commands. Her dog would be amazing.

"Why, of course, Rika." Willem nodded agreeably at his daughter's earnest request. "But you must understand that we cannot afford to buy *two* dogs, a Border Collie *and* a guard dog. We will see how things go and perhaps there will be enough for your herding dog pup next year. What do you think?"

Rika had predicted his response nearly to the word. In her mind, she had practised her arguments for getting both dogs at the same time. She had been planning and saving for her herding collie pup for over a year already.

The pup would be a female, perhaps with one blue eye and one brown, and maybe a red-and-white or tri-colour rather than the more common black-and-white dog. Her name would be Belle. She could picture her now, streaking out and around the sheep to bring them in from the field, then, on another whistle, running back out to round up the cattle as well. Belle would save Papa so much time. And she would also be a star at obedience trials and win ribbons and trophies at all the competitions.

But now Rika had to make a choice, because she knew there was not enough money for two puppies. As much as she hated the idea, she finally reconciled herself to waiting a bit longer for her Border Collie. Anyway, she knew how much time it took to train a pup by watching her friends' struggles, and Syd kept cautioning them to work with only one pup at a time.

Rika sighed. "Okay, Papa. Syd said she could come with me to visit the breeder, if that's okay with you."

"Certainly. She sounds like she knows her dogs and cats, from what you have told me."

"She knows all about sheep and cows and pigs. She specialized in farm animals at vet college. I think she should take over for Dr. Godfrey when he retires. When *will* he retire, Papa?"

"Never, I think," Willem chuckled. "Did you finish your homework already? I think we have talked enough business for one evening. It is getting late."

"What about the dishes?" Rika asked without much enthusiasm.

"My turn tonight. You hit the books, young lady!"

Rika sighed again and turned to go. "Thanks, Papa. I guess," she muttered under her breath.

The following Saturday morning, Rika waited anxiously for Syd's arrival at her farm. When she saw the burgundy truck turning into their driveway, she launched herself out the door. Syd parked next to the van Wijks' full-size grey pickup while Rika bounced on her heels.

"Hi, Syd!"

"Good morning, Rika. What a beautiful place you have here." She opened her arms wide and swept them around, her gaze admiring the view. "So neat, with the Austrian pines along the driveway, and a gorgeous century farmhouse. Just like Uncle Alistair described it."

Rika turned around to regard the tidy, white, two-storey house trimmed in dark blue. A large white dairy barn stood just behind and to the left of the house. The smaller sheep barn was nearly hidden behind the dairy barn and a row of maples just beginning to leaf out. By the end of May, the sheep barn would not be visible at all. She had never before considered her house as anything special. It was well kept and tidier than most farm homes she'd seen, now that she thought about it.

"Uh, thanks. Did you bring Megan?"

"No, I didn't think it would be a good idea. A strange dog would probably upset all the breeder's guard dogs on their own property. Especially a Border Collie."

"Oh, yeah, I didn't think of that."

Rika noticed Syd looking up, past her shoulder. Her father, wearing a clean pair of navy coveralls, had just come out of the dairy barn and was approaching them. He stretched out his hand.

"Good morning. You must be Sydney. Willem van Wijk." He introduced himself in the formal Dutch manner, nodding his head and smiling as they shook hands.

"Yes, this is Syd, Papa." Rika was embarrassed, but neither her father nor Syd seemed to notice.

"It's nice to meet you, Mr. van Wijk."

"Please call me Willem."

"Willem, then. My uncle has told me about you. He says

you have the healthiest herd of dairy cows on Prince Edward Island."

"Well, I am sure he says that about a lot of dairy farmers. It does not pay to have sick animals."

"That last part may be true, but you're wrong about a lot of farmers being as attentive as you are to herd health. You know Uncle Alistair's twisted sense of humour—says he's glad there aren't too many like you or he'd be out of business!" Syd and Willem both laughed.

Rika stared at them, uncomprehending. As far as she was concerned, Dr. Godfrey had no sense of humour whatsoever.

"So, you two ladies are off to get us a dog?" Willem asked, still smiling.

"First, we'll check out this breeder, Mrs. Brewer, and make sure she has good dogs. Are you all set to buy a dog if she has one available?" Syd looked at Rika then Willem in turn.

"Rika knows how much she can spend. If it is much more, we will have to see," Willem advised.

Rika felt a pang at the thought that it would probably be a long, long time, maybe years, before she would ever have her Border Collie pup. But this was what her sheep needed now, and what she had to do. She should be feeling excited about getting a new pup, but instead she swallowed a hard lump of regret as she and Syd climbed into the truck and started off for Guardian Angel Kennels.

Chapter Four

The clouds hung low and dark, threatening rain as Syd turned the truck off a secondary road at a sign for the kennel. They drove down a long, winding dirt driveway bordered by a thick hedge of black spruce on each side. The truck slid in and out of deep ruts in the red muck, the ground still saturated from snow melt. "Thank God for four-wheel drive," Syd muttered as the truck shuddered and climbed out of one of the deeper ruts.

Rika began to worry that they might not get back out again if they had to drive much longer. Just then, they rounded a corner and saw the house, a weathered, grey, cedar bungalow flanked by chestnut oaks at each end. Several small unpainted barns were scattered beyond the house. When they stepped out of the truck, they could hear the far-off sounds of sheep bleating, although there were none in sight. Then the barking started. First one dog, then another, then several more joined the chorus. This had to be the right place.

Mrs. Brewer, who seemed to appear from nowhere, greeted her visitors with a large, toothy smile and a vigorous handshake. "Welcome to Guardian Angel Kennels!" she boomed.

She was a short, stocky woman with straight, chin-length, steel-grey hair. Rika noticed that Mrs. Brewer's hands and feet seemed rather large for her size as she waved at them to follow her, bouncing off toward the small barns behind her house, agile and quick in spite of her chunky boots. Rika exchanged a smile with Syd as they trotted after her, imagining Mrs. Brewer as a Hobbit scurrying ahead of them.

"Marya!" she yelled when they reached the fence surrounding a kennel. From around a corner an enormous white dog bounded out and began to bark furiously when she saw them.

"Hush, Marya, these are *friends*!" Marya stopped barking at once and stood quietly on the other side of the gate, wagging her tail in a circle over her back.

"She's beautiful!" Rika was dazzled by the brilliant white coat, coal-black nose, and soft, chocolate-brown eyes. "What does *Marya* mean? Is it like the name Mary?"

"In Turkish, it means a female sheep, a ewe. Akbash Dogs come from Turkey originally."

Syd asked if Marya was safe to pet.

"Of course, Dr. Godfrey. Come on into the pen." Rika looked up in surprise to hear Syd referred to as a doctor. But that's what she was, of course: a veterinary doctor.

Mrs. Brewer continued. "Marya is well socialized. Anyway, you'll be safe as long as I'm here with you." She unlatched the gate and the three of them walked in, much to Marya's delight. Her tail whirled like a helicopter blade about to lift her off the ground. She leaned on Mrs. Brewer for a pat, then nudged Rika's hand. Rika petted the big dog's head, then scratched her behind the ears. She grinned when Marya groaned and pushed her head into Rika's hand.

Syd smiled at them. "What does she weigh, Mrs. Brewer?"

"Just shy of 100 pounds, about 45 kilos."

"That's what I weigh," Rika giggled.

"She's a fine-looking bitch," Syd commented. "Looks like she's been nursing pups."

"Yes, they're six weeks old now. We can have a peek at them in the kennel. Follow me." As she started toward the kennel building, she noticed a look of concern on Syd's face. "Don't worry about Marya. As long as you're with me, she's cool."

As they entered the building, they heard the unmistakable sounds of puppies at play—yips and growls and short, sharp barks. Inside a large pen, eight fluffy snowballs rolled and tumbled in the straw, each a miniature copy of the mother.

"Oh, they're gorgeous!"

"You're welcome to go in with them, Rika, if you're not afraid of all those sharp puppy claws and teeth. They're a wild, mouthy bunch at this age."

Rika sat in the middle and was soon covered in pups. She picked each one up and kissed them on the tops of their fuzzy heads as they mobbed her for attention. They tried to chew on her fingers and hair and clothing. She rolled on the straw, laughing as they poked and tickled her face with their wet noses and tongues. Rika was smitten.

When she finally left the pups and stood back to admire them from outside the pen, she knew she simply had to have one. Her heart pounded, and she was afraid to look Mrs. Brewer in the eyes. She had three hundred dollars saved in her puppy fund and prayed it would not be much more than that, but she knew that purebred dogs could cost over a thousand dollars.

"I guess I should ask you how much a puppy costs."

"Well, my dear, before we talk prices, I must tell you that all these pups are spoken for." She smiled with sympathy at Rika's downcast face. "I take reservations months in advance. These pups will be shipped all over North America in a few weeks."

"I hear they're still rare over here, Mrs. Brewer," Syd said.

The breeder nodded her head. "I do have another possibility, however—a proposition, if you will. Follow me," she ordered and marched them into a large outdoor run. Another huge white dog, this one with a massive head and a magnificent mane, stood two feet away, eyeing them with interest.

"Rika, Dr. Godfrey, meet Vasi the Terrible. We imported him from Turkey just two months ago." Rika and Syd had stopped at the gate, not sure if they should proceed.

"Don't be alarmed," she chuckled. "*Vasi* means guardian in Turkish, and we tacked on 'the Terrible' because he is such a sweetheart. He adores people, children in particular. We spent some time with him and the shepherds, watched them bring the sheep out of the hill country and down into the village. If he saw a dog he didn't recognize, he puffed up to twice his size and let out a roar. He looked like a friggin' big lion, he did. And believe me, that was enough to keep the other dogs away. Then once the sheep were penned up in the village, he'd go looking for children and just hang out. And he was fine with the village dogs he already knew."

Vasi approached Rika and stared up at her expectantly. She was speechless for a moment, then tentatively reached down to pet him and felt the texture of his long, coarse coat. "It feels quite different from Marya's." She looked at Mrs. Brewer. "What happened to his ears? The tips are gone. And look, there are scars on his forehead and nose. Was he in a fight?" As Rika massaged his head and ears, Vasi leaned into her. She laughed, bracing herself so he didn't push her over.

Mrs. Brewer frowned and shook her head. "Oh yes, he's seen his share of battles, mostly with other dogs. The Turkish shepherds have a custom where they often chop off the ears of their working dogs. It sounds awful,

I know, sort of like cropping the ears of Dobermans so they have a certain fierce or perky look for the show ring. I think that practice is slowly disappearing here and in Europe, isn't that so, Dr. Godfrey?"

Syd nodded her head. "Yes, it's become illegal in some places, and these days many veterinarians refuse to do any such unnecessary cosmetic surgery."

"In Turkey, the main reason they still carry on this tradition has to do with all the fights the dogs get into. When wolves or stray dogs attack the sheep, the battles to protect them can be fierce. And a dog's ears are easily shredded. They bleed a lot and are slow to heal. Sometimes dogs with intact ears injure themselves on their own spiked collars! They wear these special collars to protect their necks from the wolves' powerful jaws. I brought a few back from Turkey, but just for display. I'll show you the collars later."

Rika was kneeling next to Vasi, rubbing the battle-scarred dog under his chin like Syd had taught her to do with strange dogs. "Poor Vasi. It must have hurt, poor guy," she soothed. Vasi did not object to her caresses. In fact, he gave her cheek a big, slurpy lick.

"How old is Vasi?" Syd asked. "He doesn't seem much larger than Marya."

Mrs. Brewer scratched her head and puckered her thick black eyebrows. "We're not sure. He's at least two years old, maybe as old as four. Record-keeping seems to be more casual there. Anyway, going by his teeth and scars, he's definitely full-grown. Many of the shepherds' dogs in Turkey don't grow as large as they do here. They don't always have good access to veterinary care or optimal diets as pups."

"I suppose they also carry heavy parasite loads, which can stunt growth," Syd said.

Mrs. Brewer nodded her head. "Absolutely. But sometimes we go overboard here. Too many well-meaning owners overfeed their dogs. Anyway, we expect Vasi's pups to be larger than he is."

Rika looked up, her eyes bright. "So you plan to breed him? To Marya, maybe?"

Mrs. Brewer burst out with a throaty laugh. "That's the idea. He's a great working dog, and he'll provide some new genes to the dogs we already have in North America. We've X-rayed his hips and we know he's free from hip dysplasia, so—"

"Hip dysplasia? What's that?" Rika blurted out before she realized she had rudely cut in.

Mrs. Brewer did not seem to be bothered by the interruption. "It's a disease of the hip joint, dear. When it does happen, the dog is usually crippled and in pain whenever he tries to walk or run. And we believe it can be passed on from parents to pups, isn't that right, Dr. Godfrey?"

Syd nodded. She gave Vasi an admiring look.

"Of course, we don't want to have that fault show up in any of our pups, so it's important that all dogs we use for breeding are free of hip dysplasia. An X-ray is the only way to know for sure. In fact, Vasi got an excellent rating on his hips, so we're really tickled. Importing dogs from Turkey can be risky, so we look for sound, solid working dogs from the villages. They won't keep dogs that aren't built properly for the rigours of patrolling on all kinds of terrain. Shepherds move the flocks up to mountain pastures in the summer, then back down closer to the villages in the winter. Dogs that don't or can't do the work aren't used for breeding. Period."

"That's excellent, Mrs. Brewer," Syd said. "Sound hips are critical, especially for such a large dog. I assume Marya has been X-rayed as well."

"Certainly, got a good rating! And we also X-ray the elbows, just to make sure," Mrs. Brewer boasted. "Listen, why don't you two gals come on inside. I have some Turkish chai and almond cake waiting for us. And we can discuss a plan I have in mind. Can't do business on an empty stomach, I always say."

She turned her back on them as Rika and Syd exchanged amused glances. This was the Island country way: farm visits, whether for business or pleasure, required refreshments like cake and tea.

They followed her out of the kennel and in through the back door of her house.

Mrs. Brewer ushered them into what she called her Turkish tearoom, inviting them to sit on the large, colourful cushions arranged around a low round table in the middle. The floor was covered by several beautiful carpets woven with intricate designs in blues, reds, and golds. Their host brought out a tray with a silver teapot, silver sugar bowl and spoons, and three small glasses laced with silver filigree. The tray was set on the table next to three plates with squares of syrup-drenched almond cake. Mrs. Brewer plunked herself onto one of the cushions next to them.

"This is how they drink their chai in the Turkish countryside," she explained and poured hot tea into the three glasses, then spooned sugar into her own. "They usually use sugar cubes in Turkey. I had to drink a lot of chai before the shepherds would talk to me about their dogs. And there weren't many toilet facilities in the rural villages where I travelled, so it was a real gut-buster, if you know what I mean." She chortled and sipped her tea.

"Mrs. Brewer, did you bring these carpets back from Turkey?" Syd asked.

"Yes, I did. Aren't they spectacular?" She looked around with a satisfied expression. "They tell me that the finest weaving is done by girls or women with small hands. Turkey is a fascinating country. The people are so generous and hospitable. The country folk don't have much, but they share what they have. At the very least, they offer you chai. A lot of them make *ayran*, which is a little like buttermilk. Very nice, too, unless you're lactose intolerant like I am, which is not a good scene, if you know what I mean. You gotta travel with your own toilet paper, too, let me tell ya!" She belted out another hearty laugh and encouraged her guests to eat their cake.

"And these must be the dog collars you mentioned." Syd pointed to several lengths of rusty iron links with spikes, hanging on a wall.

"Ah, yes. It's common to see them on the active working dogs. They're also worn by stock dogs in eastern and southern Europe. Think of them as part of a uniform, or armour for soldiers going into battle. As you can see, the spikes point out. Vasi almost impaled me on one of those. He's so friendly, he just wanted to cuddle up to me wearing an iron collar. Not!" she said in her big voice, making Rika jump and slip partway off her silk cushion.

"Remind me to show you my belly dancing costume before you go. Red satin with silver spangles. To die for! Got it in the Grand Bazaar in Istanbul. On a dare, you understand. Then when I got back home, I heard they started belly dance classes in Charlottetown. It's a great way to exercise, I might just go." She looked up to see Rika's eyes wide and mouth hanging open. "No, not wearing the costume!" She roared with laughter as Rika, blushing, shut her mouth and lowered her head to take another sip of tea.

"Anyway," she continued, "back to business. Since you live here on the Island, Rika, and you are looking for a dog to guard your sheep, I'd like to make a proposal." She paused and looked directly at Rika. "You did tell me you had electric fencing around your sheep pastures, didn't you?" Her tone was almost accusing.

"Yes, six strands. But it didn't keep the coyotes out." Rika worried that she was giving the wrong answer.

"To me that's not as important as keeping animals in. Anyway, I wondered if you might be interested in taking Vasi home with you and putting him to work with your flock. He knows all about electric fencing. He wouldn't dream of trying to go over, under, or through it!"

Rika stared at Mrs. Brewer, her jaw slack with surprise. "I—I don't think we can afford an imported dog. I know they cost a lot—"

"No, no," Mrs. Brewer interrupted her, shaking her head and waving her free hand. "I'm not selling him. I would like to keep Vasi nearby so we can use him as a stud dog. If he lived on your farm, he could protect your sheep and still be close enough we could borrow him from time to time for breeding purposes. If you prefer, we could work out a co-ownership arrangement. I really believe Vasi would be happier living with sheep than hanging out in a large pen by himself."

"Don't you have livestock, Mrs. Brewer?" Syd asked. "I hear the coyotes are thick in this part of the island."

"You betcha they are. And we already have three dogs guarding our sheep and goats. We don't actually need Vasi's guardian skills here on our farm at the moment. Anyway, it's a bit tricky introducing adult dogs to each other. I'm concerned about them fighting, because they are strangers and they may feel too crowded in our pastures. We already have one alpha male, and I suspect Vasi would challenge him for that position. It would be best if we found a separate working situation for Vasi. Do you want to think about it and let me know?"

Rika looked down at her hands clutching the tea glass. She did not know what to say. After seeing the pups, she'd been totally won over and knew that was what she wanted. "I'll need to talk to my father. What do you think, Syd?"

"It's your call, Rika, but it does sound like a good deal for everybody. Anyway, we should talk to your dad first, and then you can let Mrs. Brewer know, okay?"

"Okay."

"I saw the kiss Vasi gave you, Rika. He doesn't do that with just anybody." Mrs. Brewer nodded her approval. "I do believe he rather likes you, dear."

Normally, Rika would have been flattered, but now she was confused and even annoyed. This was not what she had expected.

Rika knew her father would appreciate the offer made by Mrs. Brewer, especially since it would cost them nothing but dog food. Syd thought it was a good plan: a ready-made guardian dog, without all the trouble of training a new pup, a process that could take two to three years. Syd also reminded her that this breed was independent-minded and not easy to train. Deaf as a haddock when they decided not to respond to commands, according to Mrs. Brewer. The mature, trained dog would have appealed to her mother, who used to handle all the farm business dealings. A win-win situation, she liked to say. But Rika's heart had been set on a puppy, and she was certain she could raise one.

"You can still have a puppy, Rika," Willem suggested after Syd had gone home. "If you have enough money set aside, perhaps you can buy that Border Collie puppy now."

But Rika dug her heels in. She had become determined to raise an Akbash puppy once she had seen them at Guardian Angel Kennels. She came up with another scheme. She would keep Vasi until Mrs. Brewer had another litter, then she could buy one of those pups.

"And would you send Vasi back to Mrs. Brewer?"

"Well, Papa, we can keep Vasi until the puppy is trained and old enough to guard on his own. By then, maybe someone else with sheep would like to keep him for Mrs. Brewer. Or maybe she will need him herself."

Willem sighed. "Daughter, you were born with your mother's stubborn nature. And so practical, too. I suppose if you can convince Mrs. Brewer to go along with this plan, then go ahead. But if she agrees, it will be some time before you can afford that Border Collie pup. Those Akbash Dogs cost nearly as much as a good Holstein heifer calf!"

Rika beamed. All thoughts of Border Collies had vanished when she first saw the white fluff balls at Guardian Angel Kennels. She was on a new path now.

Chapter Five

Rika had no stomach for breakfast the morning Mrs. Brewer arranged to bring Vasi over to Willemrika Farm. Anticipating the anxiety, her father had made her favourite: French toast with maple syrup and vanilla yogurt.

"Rika, try to eat something, just half a piece. Please," he urged.

"I can't, Papa, I'm too excited," she admitted, her stomach in knots. She hadn't slept well—another bloody nightmare had haunted her. What if the sheep didn't accept Vasi? What if he chased them? What if he got out of the fence and onto the road? She had a lot of worries, but Rika did not share them with her father, because she knew what he would say: "Stay calm, everything will be fine." She could only think of the many things that might go wrong.

She especially missed her mother at times like this. Ingrid van Wijk would listen to all of Rika's concerns, no matter how serious or silly, and still manage to calm her agitated daughter. She'd had a way of absorbing all the darkness in Rika's life and emitting lightness and peace. At least, that's how Rika remembered her.

The rumbling of a car engine had Rika running to the kitchen window. "Oh, she's here, Papa!" she shouted, and ran for her boots.

Willem shook his head and followed.

When Rika peered into the open truck window, she was surprised and delighted to see that Vasi sat on the passenger seat next to Mrs. Brewer, not in the back of the pickup. Vasi calmly surveyed his surroundings, as if accustomed to taking rides in the front seat.

"Good morning, Mrs. Brewer. Hello, Vasi!"

"Good morning, Rika. Lovely day, isn't it?" Mrs. Brewer clipped a leash to Vasi's collar. She opened her door and he followed her obediently out of the driver's side. When Vasi landed on the ground next to Rika, his tail broke into his distinctive circular wag.

"He's smiling at you, Rika," Mrs. Brewer said with a broad grin. "You have a beautiful, neat farm here. I wish my place was as nicely kept. Ah, you must be Mr. van Wijk. So pleased to meet you!" She stretched out her hand to Willem, who stood behind Rika.

"Would you like to come in for some coffee?" Willem offered.

"Oh no, not now, thank you. Perhaps later. We should introduce Vasi to his new flock, if you don't mind. Dogs first. Which way?"

As soon as he heard the baaing sheep near the barn, Vasi began to strain on his leash.

"Look at how keen he is," Mrs. Brewer said. "He hasn't been with sheep for over two months now, and I believe he misses them. Of course, your sheep may not be so happy to see him, especially after the coyote attack."

When they walked into the barn, the sheep bawled even louder. For them, people usually meant food. But when they saw Vasi, the baaing ceased abruptly, as if a conductor had just rapped his baton. Several ewes stomped their front feet and lowered their heads.

Vasi whined. "No, Vasi," Mrs. Brewer said in a quiet voice. "You have to let them get used to you. Easy now," she soothed him. "Here, Rika, take the leash. The sheep don't know me, either. Walk up to them with Vasi, but stop about five feet away and tell Vasi to lie down." She handed the leash to the anxious girl, and Willem opened the gate for her. Then he and Mrs. Brewer stood back and watched.

Rika and Vasi approached the sheep slowly. His tail wagged furiously over his back, a flag hailing new comrades. The ewes did not recognize his overtures of friendship and stomped their feet with more insistence. Vasi understood the signal and lowered his tail, still wagging the tip, still hopeful. The ewes jostled and crowded into the farthest corner away from the dog. Five feet from the flock, Rika stopped.

"Lie down, Vasi," she commanded. Vasi looked up at her, then at the sheep, and yawned. Rika knew from dog classes that a yawn did not mean he was tired—he simply did not wish to obey her instructions. "Down, Vasi!" she commanded in the loud, firm tone she'd heard Syd using. With reluctance Vasi lowered his front end, looked at Rika once more, sighed, then lay down completely, resting his head on his paws.

"Good boy," she praised him in a soft voice so he would not get too excited.

"I think he'll be okay, Rika," Mrs. Brewer said. "Why don't you sit next to him for a while and give the sheep a chance to check him out?"

Not long after Rika sat down, two ewes approached them. Nosy and Grumpy were the nicknames she'd given her two original and oldest ewes. They were also the most curious and boldest. Rika could feel Vasi trembling next to her. His tail rustled in the straw behind them, stirring up dust. The two ewes finally halted within a few inches of Vasi, sniffing and still stomping their feet. Nosy took the plunge and touched Vasi's nose. Immediately his big tongue slipped out to lick her face. She jumped back in surprise, startling Grumpy, and they both ran back to the flock.

They repeated this manoeuvring for ten minutes or so, back and forth, until the two ewes had nibbled on Vasi's back and head, satisfying themselves about the identity and safety of the stranger. They returned to the flock and continued to stare at him.

"That's a good start," said Mrs. Brewer. "Why don't you release him now? As long as the ewes are wary of him, he'll keep his distance and won't bug them. Vasi is a sensible dog."

Rika unsnapped his leash and stood up. Vasi didn't budge.

"I'll have that coffee now," Mrs. Brewer said to Willem.

"Certainly. Rika, will you come in with us, or do you plan to supervise in here?"

"I'm staying." Rika wondered how he could possibly imagine she would leave at such a critical time. She sat on a bale of hay, out of the way, so she could watch the interactions between the sheep and dog. She felt sorry for Vasi, who wanted so much to be accepted by the sheep. Still, she understood why her sheep were so cautious after the horrible experience they'd had with coyotes. This could take some time.

Within two days, the sheep had completely accepted Vasi's presence and were treating him like a member of the flock. Rika marvelled at their trust. She was now able to let them back on the pasture and into the area where the coyote attack had occurred. Her father assured Rika that Blaine Doiron had removed all the traps.

One evening later that week, Rika and Willem were eating their supper when they heard Vasi's unmistakable barking, only more intense and high-pitched than usual.

"Papa, may I be excused? I have to see what Vasi's barking at," she pleaded.

"I am sure he has everything under control, Rika," Willem suggested. "You are almost finished eating—"

"Papa, I can't eat another bite! Please!"

He sighed. "Very well, go."

Rika launched herself from the table and practically straight into her boots, not bothering with overalls. She was out the door and racing down the pasture faster than Willem, who watched from the doorway, had ever seen before.

From a distance, Rika saw the sheep huddled in the same area where the coyote kill had occurred. "Oh no, not again. Please don't let it be!" she prayed out loud, panting hard and feeling her heart would explode.

When she reached the sheep, they were all gathered behind Vasi, who stood as close to the electric fence as he dared without actually touching it. He did not want to get bitten by the fence wires, as Mrs. Brewer would say. Instead, he whined and barked at something outside the fence. His tail was curled high up over his back in the alert position, but still wagging. He pranced back and forth, acting like he wanted to get to the other side.

Rika stopped next to him, breathing hard from her run, and stared into the bushes. "What is it, Vasi? What's out there?"

As soon as she spoke, high-pitched bleating broke out from the bushes, and two noses poked into view. Her lambs! "How in the world did you get out there?" Rika looked up and down the fence line to see if there were any broken wires. Everything seemed to be intact. As she walked along the fence in one direction, the flock followed her. When she turned and walked the other way, they did the same, her Velcro sheep.

Then she noticed a bit of wool on the lowest strand

of wire. It was in the place where she, Liz, and Stirling had gone under the fence to look for the trapped coyote. Who said sheep were stupid? She knew that lambs were curious about new things, and the wool on their backs had probably insulated them from the shock when they slipped under the wire. She would have to test the fence to make sure the electric charger was still working properly. Then she would have to plug up that hollow so the lambs couldn't scoot under any more. But first, she had to figure out how to lure the lambs back inside the pasture before any coyotes discovered them.

"Here sheep, sheep," she coaxed the rest of the flock. "Come with me and get some grain. I know it's a bit early, but perhaps our Houdini lambs will follow if we all go. Come along, sheep, sheep!" It seemed to work. The ewes turned their attention from the wayward lambs towards Rika, their food dispenser. Vasi wasn't convinced by this ploy. He lay down next to the fence and whined.

"Vasi, come on!" Rika urged. "If you stay, the lambs won't need to get back in. Vasi, come!" she commanded in her best Mrs. Brewer voice. Vasi ignored her. "Are you growing potatoes in your ears?" This was what Liz's mother said to get the attention of her youngsters.

Rika finally decided to continue to the barn with the rest of the flock. She would pen them inside, turn off the power to the fence, then grab a leash. Vasi weighed as much as she did, but he was obedient on leash. At least, he had been up to now. As she locked the ewes inside the barn, leash in hand, she decided on plan B, in case plan A didn't work.

"Papa?" she called, poking her head into the kitchen. "Could you come to the pasture with me? Two of the lambs are on the other side of the fence and Vasi won't leave them, and they won't come back in." Rika paused to catch her breath. "The rest of the flock is in the barn already."

"Oh, really?" Willem appeared from the living room, newspaper in hand. "Perhaps they will follow you if you bring Vasi back. I see you have his leash."

Rika hated to ask for help; the sheep were her responsibility. But this time, in case Vasi did not cooperate, she might need backup. "Well, Papa—"

"Aha!" Willem grinned and pointed out the door, behind her. "What do I see?"

Rika turned and stared in disbelief. Vasi was calmly trotting back from the lower pasture, the two lambs zigzagging along behind him.

"Oh," she muttered. "Plan C, I guess."

Willem looked at her, his eyebrows up.

"I'd better fix that hole in the fence," she said, and left without explaining.

"Good dog," Willem said, and returned to the living room to read his evening paper.

Chapter Six

"Syd, can you have a look at Vasi? He's been coughing and panting a lot and it doesn't sound right." Rika's brow was furrowed. Dr. Godfrey and Syd had just finished working with Bianca, one of the older dairy cows. Bianca had given birth to a huge bull calf but was unable to stand to let him nurse. Rika was delighted that Dr. Godfrey had brought Syd along. She'd been concerned about Vasi lately, but she didn't want to bother Mrs. Brewer.

"Sure, Rika," Syd said. "I'll have a look at Vasi. Let me wash up first."

"Dr. Godfrey senior, would you stop for some coffee while Dr. Godfrey junior examines the dog?" Willem offered with the hint of a smile.

"Oh, I suppose." The elder veterinarian grumbled and shuffled off with his host. "Senior indeed!"

The sheep were nearby, so Vasi was already at the fence watching Syd and Rika approach. Once inside the pasture, the happy dog greeted them with his circular tail wags and heavy, raspy panting.

"You're right, Rika, his breathing isn't normal." Syd took out her stethoscope and knelt next to Vasi. She placed the end piece against his chest. "Put your hands around his muzzle and close his mouth while I listen to his lungs and heart."

Syd listened as she moved the stethoscope over Vasi's chest and rib cage. "His heart is working much too hard. Has he been running this morning?"

Rika shook her head. "He doesn't even run after the barn cats anymore."

Syd gave Rika a questioning look. "He used to chase them?"

"Yeah, at first he did, but I don't think he would ever hurt them. Now they walk right up to him and rub on his legs, and it doesn't bother him."

"He knows the cats belong here now, I suppose. Does he ever run for any reason?"

"He still runs after the crows," Rika said, then frowned. "That's when I hear him coughing, after he's chased them off."

Syd removed the earpieces of her stethoscope and stood up, looking concerned. "Rika, I think we should take him in for some tests. I'm going to ask Mrs. Brewer what medical history she might have from when he first came to Canada."

"What kind of tests?" Rika asked and knelt down to give Vasi a hug.

"Looking for parasites would be a good place to start."

"Parasites? But Mrs. Brewer said she wormed him just before he left her farm."

"Sure, for the parasites we have here on PEI. But in countries like Turkey they have all kinds of different types, some that live inside and some on the outside of dogs. And sheep, too. I'm thinking maybe lungworms, or heartworms."

"Are those serious?" Rika could feel a knot growing in her stomach.

"They don't have to be. Anyway, dogs can be treated for them. All we need is a blood test and maybe a chest X-ray."

They closed the gate and walked toward the house.

Rika tugged at her hair, more anxious than ever. "Are those tests expensive?"

"Oh, they might cost forty or fifty dollars each, but Mrs. Brewer has agreed to pay all veterinary expenses, remember?"

"Yeah, I know. But what if she thinks I'm not taking good care of Vasi? What if she wants to take him back?" The thought of losing Vasi suddenly frightened her.

Syd smiled warmly and put her arm around the girl's shoulders. "Rika, you are such a worrier. If he has heartworm, it won't be your fault, or even Mrs. Brewer's."

Rika shrugged, but the worry did not leave her. She had been surprised at how quickly the big white dog fit in with her flock. The fact that the sheep trusted him so soon after his arrival was also amazing. This breed was so unlike all the Border Collies she knew. Collies yearned for constant attention and watched their owners intently for any possibility of play or work. Vasi was pleased to see Rika, and of course he loved to be fed and petted. But once she left, he was content to lie peacefully with the sheep or patrol the pastures. Whenever she looked into his calm dark eyes, she felt that he was in charge, that she could depend on him. If Rika was in one of her worried or frantic states of mind, just rubbing his ears or running her hands through his thick coat eased her anxiety. She would leave feeling content. Vasi was growing on her.

Now she dreaded the thought that he might be seriously ill. She could feel her eyes fill up, but she held back the tears. As they reached the house, Syd gave Rika a hug, and whispered, "He'll be okay."

Rika gave a deep sigh. She felt a little better as she waved good-bye to Syd and Dr. Godfrey.

Rika needed to study for final exams that week, but she had a hard time concentrating. She slept poorly, still fretting about how sick Vasi might be. His tests were scheduled for the following day, and Syd had promised to take the blood samples and deliver them to the laboratory herself.

When Rika arrived home from school, Vasi was still at the clinic. She burst into the house and called for her father.

"Did you hear yet? Are the tests finished?" she demanded when she found him sitting at the computer, working on the farm accounting.

Willem calmly pushed the save button before he turned to the agitated girl at his side. "Ya, the tests are complete and Syd guessed correctly. Vasi has a heartworm infection."

"Oh, no!" Rika wailed, putting her hands on her cheeks and sinking to the floor beside him.

"Now, Rika, no need for such dramatics. He will be treated and cured. You do trust Syd's judgement, yes?"

Rika nodded her head.

"Remember how she noticed the udder on Thea? She just walked by, and knew what the problem was right away. She is a sharp one, that Dr. Godfrey junior. I am certain she will get Vasi through this."

Rika kept nodding her head, her lips pressed together.

He continued. "Syd said she would start treatment right away. They need to keep him in the clinic, under observation. The drug they use to kill the heartworm can be hard on the liver, so they will take blood samples twice a day to make sure his body is reacting well. If not, they will stop the treatment and try again in a few weeks' time." Willem patted the drooping head next to him as tears filled her eyes.

"Poor Vasi. Can I visit him?"

"He needs to stay quiet during the treatment, so Syd said it would be best not to get him excited with visits.

He might think he is coming home if you went to see him. Think how upset he might be each time you left him."

"I could stay with him all the time," she suggested.

"What about your exams?" Willem asked. "Who is going to do them for you?"

"Papa, I can't study anyway."

"Well, give it a try. If it makes you feel better, call Syd so she can give you all the details." He paused. "Vasi is going to be fine."

"Oh, Papa, I hope so," Rika whispered and wiped away her tears. "I guess we'd better keep the sheep at the barn until he comes home." Back to where they started, she thought.

The next two days were uneventful at home and in the clinic. Syd reported daily and told Rika that Vasi was holding up well. By the third day, Rika was preoccupied with exams, so she did not question her father when he told her that Syd had called earlier to say everything was still okay. On Thursday Rika wrote her final exam for the semester. Afterward, she had arranged to go to Liz's home to celebrate with a few of their friends, and Willem agreed to take care of her sheep chores so she could spend the night at Liz's place. He promised to call her with any new developments concerning Vasi.

Once their friends had left and Liz's younger brothers and sisters were in bed, the two girls headed for the computer. Liz's older brother Charlie was playing a computer game. "Charlie, you said we could use the computer at ten. It's five after," Liz reminded him.

"Okay, okay, almost done. There, ha, won again!" He turned off his game and grinned at the girls. "All warmed up for you. That keyboard is hot!" Charlie jumped up and danced out of the room. He stuck his head back in as Liz was logging on. "Did you leave me any chips for the salsa?"

"Yeah, yeah, there's a bag in the back of the cupboard," Liz said without turning around. "Here, Rika, you can log on now."

Rika slipped into the chair while Liz sat on a stool next to her. Finally, she could check her email. No one knew about her Hotmail account except for Liz, a couple of friends from school, and her cousin Elly. There were three messages from her friends, and two from her cousin.

She read Elly's email messages aloud to Liz, like she always did, thinking of her cousin as an older sister they both shared. "I can't believe what she gets away with," Rika commented when she finished. "If only Aunt Martina knew half of what she does. That must be her fourth boyfriend this year."

"Is she seventeen or eighteen?"

"Almost seventeen, and her parents are nearly as strict as Papa. The parties she goes to are wild, and her parents have no idea." Rika shook her head.

"Sounds a lot like Charlie's friend Wally, who's a total idiot, especially when he's drunk. Much better when they're all smoking pot." Liz paused and wound a curly strand of hair around her index finger. "Vasi's coming home tomorrow, isn't he?"

"Yeah," Rika replied. "I sure hope he'll be okay after everything he's been through."

The next morning, Liz's mother dropped Rika off at home. She burst through the front door, shouting for her father. She found him at the kitchen table. "Are we going to get Vasi?"

"And good day to you, too, young lady. Did you have fun last night?" He smiled at her impatience.

"Uh-huh, it was great. What about Vasi?" Rika was not to be put off.

"Syd will drop him off later this evening," he said,

lowering his eyes, his smile evaporating. "Rika, I must tell you something about Vasi."

"What?" she practically screamed, recognizing his veiled look. She had seen that same expression five years before when he'd broken the news about her mother's fatal accident. "What happened to him?"

Willem put his hands on Rika's shoulders. "Rika, Vasi is fine. He is okay for now, and he will be home later," he said in a level voice, still holding on to her shaking form. "What I wanted to say, is he started to have a bad reaction, so Syd stopped the treatment. He will have a rest, then they will start treatment again in a month. The second time around, his liver will be used to the drug, so it can kill the parasites without harming him."

Rika pushed his hands from her shoulders and stared at her father. "So you lied to me! You told me everything was fine. Why did you lie to me?" she demanded, her hands on her hips, her blue eyes blazing.

"You get so worked up about the smallest things, Rika. I wanted you to concentrate on your exams. Anyway, nothing bad happened. Vasi will be fine, I told you."

"And why didn't Syd call me, like she said she would? Every day. She promised."

Willem sighed. "Do not blame Syd. I asked her not to. I just wanted to see you get through the week, that is all. I am sorry if you are upset." He started for the door, then stopped and turned around. "And there is something else I must tell you."

"Oh? What?" In spite of being annoyed with her father, Rika was curious. She couldn't imagine him giving her two doses of bad news at one time.

"Um... Syd and I are planning to go to a movie tonight." He paused and looked down for a moment. "I hope you will not mind being on your own this evening. Call Liz over if you like."

Rika's mouth dropped open in shock. Syd and Papa? How could he? How could she? Her father had not dated anyone since her mother had died. She stomped out of the room without saying a word.

Inside her bedroom, Rika felt tears of exasperation burning her cheeks. Her mother was gone—gone forever. She had been to the funeral, she had watched her father grieving. She had seen them lowering her mother's casket into the ground. A lovely white marble headstone marked the grave, with her mother's name, the years she was born and died engraved under an angel.

The last time Rika had seen her mother, she had driven off on a wintry night, over treacherous, icy roads, to visit a sick friend. Ingrid van Wijk had trained as a nurse in Holland, but she never practised that profession in Canada. Instead, along with keeping the farm accounts, she nurtured the animals on their farm and became a local resource for friends with health concerns and minor ailments.

For a year after her mother's death, Rika had the feeling, the hope, that Ingrid would return, that perhaps the person in the casket was not her mother. The casket had remained shut; no one was allowed to see the body. They told her the car had slipped off the road and rolled several times down a cliff, smashing on the rocky beach below. It was best to remember her mother as she'd been before the crash, they said.

But what if there was no one in the casket at all and it was an elaborate cover-up? Maybe her mother was on a secret mission as an international spy, and the government had set it up to look like she was dead. She'd heard of this happening before.

As the years passed, she had pushed those childish musings aside. Her mother was not coming back, ever. And yet, tucked away in a small, dark corner of her mind, like a tiny, unlit tea light buried in a hope chest, was a glimmer of possibility. Never give up, it whispered.

And now her father had stopped waiting. He was going on a date.

When Syd arrived with Vasi later that evening, she acted cheerful, like nothing had changed. Rika felt awkward, as if Syd had morphed into a total stranger.

"How is Vasi? Can he go out with the sheep?" was all she wanted to know.

"Sure, he can go right back to work," Syd replied. "Let's go get him."

Rika followed her out to her truck, where Vasi waited patiently in a large crate in the back. Syd opened the crate and snapped a leash to his collar and he sprang to the ground. She handed the leash to Rika, who turned immediately toward the barn.

"You don't mind if we go out to see a movie, do you, Rika?" she called out in the dark.

"I don't care." Rika shrugged but did not look back, did not say good-bye. She was being rude, but she couldn't help herself.

Inside the barn, she let Vasi loose and watched him sniff around, his tail wagging with quick strokes over his back. Rika opened a gate and he bounced through to greet the sheep, who startled and scattered away from him. Then they stopped, turned around, and stared at him. Vasi slowed to a walk but continued to approach them, his head and tail lowered. Once he was allowed to touch noses with Nosy and Grumpy, he circled the flock and bounded out into the pasture. Rika watched him lift his leg against certain fence posts, sniff the ground, and continue his rounds. Finally, he returned to the ewes and lay down near them, satisfied all was well in his domain.

"Well, I'm glad *you're* happy, Vasi," Rika muttered. She

stayed at the barn until she heard the truck engine start up and she knew Syd and her father had left.

As soon as she was back inside the house, she telephoned Liz. "Hey, Liz. What're you doing tonight?"

"Babysitting the brats, as usual. They're watching a video, it's not too bad yet. Did you get your dog back?"

"Yeah, he's back. They couldn't finish his treatment because he had a bad reaction, so they have to do it again in a month. Papa knew it the whole time and never told me! But that's not the worst news." She paused.

"What?" Liz's squeal stabbed her ear through the receiver.

Although Liz was her best friend and they shared all their secrets, Rika found herself hesitating. She actually felt embarrassed about telling her.

"What's going on?" Liz asked again.

"My dad went out with Syd," she blurted.

"Huh? Where did they go?"

"To a movie. They went to a movie together!"

"Oh, you mean they're on a date? Ooh, sweet," she said. "Jess, pipe down! I'm on the phone!" she shouted at a brother.

Rika began to feel irritated. Sometimes her best friend could be so dense. There was nothing sweet about her father on a date with someone she considered *her* friend.

"So, what's the bad news?"

"Didn't you hear what I just said? My dad and Syd. It's too weird, it doesn't seem right. I don't know—"

"Jess, give it back to him!" Liz shouted. "Well, why not, Rika?" she continued in a quieter voice. "Syd's really nice, she's smart, she's pretty. I love her hair. I wish I had auburn hair, it's so amazing. I'm going to put red henna in my hair this weekend. That's what Gail did to hers, and I think it turned out great. Did you notice it?"

"No, I didn't. And who cares, anyway? Gail is always

doing stuff to her hair—it's different every day. I'm talking about Syd, not Gail."

"Well, I wish I had red hair. Or blond. Anything but this boring brown colour. You and your dad have gorgeous hair. You know, your dad is really good-looking. I'll bet a lot of women would like to go out with him. Georgia thought he was your older brother, remember? *She* wanted to go out with him!" Liz laughed, then stopped abruptly. "Oh great, I just heard a big crash. I've gotta go. I don't know what they're up to now, but it sounds expensive, and *I'm* going to get in trouble. Talk to you later." She hung up.

"Yeah," Rika muttered to herself. What was the big deal, anyway? Her dad could have been going out with all sorts of women if he wanted to. But why did he have to pick Syd? And why now? Syd was *her* friend. Or she used to be. Maybe, she thought, Syd asked her father out. Rika had looked up to Syd. How could she do something like this to her?

Still early evening, Rika decided to take her book to bed and read until she heard her father return. Then she would shut off her light. She was not in the mood for a bedtime chat tonight.

Chapter Seven

Rika was drying breakfast dishes the following Saturday when she heard a car drive up. She looked out the window to see three boys tumbling out of Stirling Howatt's family car. Billy Miller was the first one out.

"Oh, no," she moaned when she noticed that Errol Keir was right behind him. And here she was, in an old shirt and sweatpants, her stringy hair tied back with an elastic band. Definitely not presentable. Rika heard her father greeting Stirling's dad outside and ran into her bedroom to change clothes.

She heard the front door open. "Rika!" her father shouted. "You have company!"

"Just a minute!" she answered and tripped over a pair of sneakers in front of her closet. She found a clean black T-shirt featuring a rock group from Holland, and she pulled on her new, still-unfaded blue jeans, the only pair of pants that weren't too short on her. She ripped the elastic out of her hair, whimpering as a few strands were yanked out with it. Finally, she knew she had to go outside and face them.

"Hello, Mr. Howatt." Rika addressed the senior person first, as she had been taught. She couldn't think of what to say to the boys, so she glanced at them briefly and raised her hand in a silent greeting. She felt her face redden.

What in the world was Errol Keir doing at her farm?

"Good morning, Rika." Mr. Howatt gave her a pleasant smile. "Stirling's been talking about this dog of yours. Do you mind if we have a look at him?" Melvin Howatt had the same dark features as his son, and his blue eyes always hinted at mischief. He was a dairy farmer, like her father, but broadly built and at least six inches shorter than Willem.

"Sure," Rika agreed and turned to walk toward the sheep pasture without looking at any of the boys.

"So has he killed any coyotes yet?" Billy asked.

"Nope," she answered without turning around.

"What does he do?" he persisted.

"Oh, nothing much. Just hangs around the sheep, sleeps most of the day. But at night he's busy, patrolling the fences, peeing on posts." She expected to get a rise out of the boys, and she wasn't disappointed when they snickered.

"Excuse me?" Errol asked, sounding very serious. "Is this perimeter peeing part of his job?" The other two boys guffawed.

Rika slowly turned around to face them. With her most serious face, she said, "Why, yes, that's how guard dogs mark their territory. That's what keeps the coyotes away. That's why they don't have to kill anything, because coyotes recognize the scent and they're smart enough to know it's trouble." She smiled at Stirling and Billy, who stared back, their jaws slack and mouths open.

Errol nodded, grinning. "That makes sense," he said. "Coyotes are in the same family as dogs, so they recognize signals left by dog urine. Whoa, is that him? He's huge! Look at the head on that guy!" They all stood at a fence outside the sheep pasture, watching Vasi bound toward them, tail held high and curled over his back.

"That's some dog!" Mr. Howatt exclaimed. "How much does he weigh?"

"About a hundred pounds."

"Why, I'll wager that's more than you, young lady," he laughed. "I hope he minds you well. Is he mean at all?"

"No, he likes people," Rika answered. "Mrs. Brewer— she's the lady who brought him here from Turkey—she says he wouldn't bite unless his sheep were threatened. But he doesn't like strange dogs."

"I imagine a dog like that would protect you, too," Mr. Howatt suggested.

"Yeah, Rika's just another sheep to him," Stirling smirked. Rika scowled and noticed Errol rolling his eyes. She tried not to smile.

"That's a baa-a-d joke, Stirling," she couldn't resist saying.

Errol gave Rika a thumbs-up, and everyone laughed except Stirling.

"Well, he's a fine-looking dog, Rika," Mr. Howatt said. "Looking at those scars, I'd say he's done some battles. Think I'll just stay on this side of the fence." Then he addressed the boys. "I need to talk to Willem a few minutes about that milking machine. We shouldn't be long."

Vasi stood on the other side of the fence, enjoying the attention even if he was not being petted. His tail continued to wag, and his tongue hung out. He almost appeared to be grinning.

"I think he has a kind face," Errol appraised, tilting his head to one side. Rika felt her heart flutter, as if he had complimented her personally.

"I think he's kind of homely," Billy said. "Those ears are weird. They give him a scary look."

"Does he do obedience?" Stirling asked.

"I haven't done any training with him, but he knows his name and comes when you call him. Most of the time, anyway. He knows *sit* and *down*, but he's pretty slow at it, nothing like the collies. I don't think he cares much about commands."

"Well, then, he can't be very smart. Border Collies are the most intelligent dogs there are," Stirling said. The Howatts' Border Collie, Crosby, rounded up their cattle at home and was one of the best obedience dogs in Syd's class.

Rika stared at him. She wanted desperately to say something witty, but she didn't know enough about Akbash Dogs to debate Stirling. She wished Mrs. Brewer was there to back her up. "So what makes an intelligent dog?" Errol broke the tense silence. "Learning tricks and commands? Or knowing how to outfox coyotes?" He winked at Rika and her heart gave another jump.

"Border Collies can do all that stuff!" Stirling bragged.

"Give me a break!" Rika said. "You're saying they can guard sheep? You know they'd rather chase and bite—they're sheep killers!"

"Crosby doesn't kill sheep!" Stirling protested.

"Because he hasn't had a chance to. Have you ever left him alone with sheep? Day and night? I bet if you left him alone with the cows, he'd run them into Prince County." Rika was incensed, and embarrassed at her outburst in front of Errol.

"Stirling! Boys! The bus is leaving," Mr. Howatt shouted from the dairy barn.

Stirling glared at Rika while Billy smirked. Errol gave her an apologetic look, and said, "See ya, thanks."

She nodded her head, afraid to say another word, and turned for the house. Rika was mortified at the impression she must have made. She stood just inside her door watching them pile back into the car. Errol looked back toward the house for a moment before he also disappeared. For some reason, she felt like crying. Why had she let Stirling get to her like that? Why had she acted like such an idiot in front of Errol? Boys!

Chapter Eight

Willem and Syd were seeing each other at least once a week, but Rika had not spoken to her father about his dating. He simply told her when and where and how long he was planning to go out so she knew when he'd be back at home. Rika was uneasy about this state of affairs, but she could not fully explain why. She chose not to discuss it with anyone, not even Liz. When she ran into two other girls in town one day she was mortified when they asked what she thought about her father's romance. She shrugged and said, "My dad can hang out with anyone he wants. It's a free country." The girls gave Rika a strange look and moved on.

Later, at home, she called Liz. "Did you tell Lucy or Carol about my dad dating?"

"No! I never said a word to anyone!" she protested. "But Mom knows about it and I never breathed a word to her. Rika, get used to it. You can't keep secrets like that on PEI, especially in the country."

So the summer ambled on, warm and breezy as Prince Edward Island summers are known to be. The pastures were lush and green with white clover, timothy, and rye grasses. Rika's lambs were finally weaned from their mothers and growing well. But what a commotion on weaning day. Vasi appeared distressed by the lambs' and ewes' non-stop bawling over the next three days. Being an athletic dog, he hopped the wooden gates between the two groups, trying to console mothers and babies. By the time everyone had settled down, he was exhausted—the heartworm infection continued to take its toll.

By mid-July, Vasi was due for his second round of treatment. This time, Rika was allowed to visit Vasi at the clinic. Each day after morning chores were done, Willem drove her there, ten kilometres from their farm. She crawled into the cage with Vasi and sat with him on a special cushion. The cage was spacious enough for Vasi to move around in, but not to jump or run. They needed to keep him still and quiet while the medicine killed the long worms that wound through his blood vessels, into and out of his heart and lungs. Rika sat with him, stroking his head and ears, massaging his legs, back, and belly. Vasi seemed content with his head on her lap, sighing deeply, his tail thumping out a rhythm on the floor of the cage.

On the fourth day of treatment, Rika sat as usual with Vasi. She was telling him about how the sheep liked to chase the barn cats out of the pasture now he wasn't there to protect them. She also mentioned how the cats missed having him inside the barn to curl up with when he took naps. She was feeling a bit sleepy herself when she heard the door to the ward open and saw a pair of legs shuffle to the cage where she sat. Then a grey head peered into the cage and they both gave a startled, "Oh!"

"What're you doin' in there, girl?" grunted old Dr. Godfrey.

"Syd said I could visit Vasi for a while. Sh-she said it was okay."

"She did, did she? Well, I think you better get on outta there until we clear somethin' up. Come on." He opened the cage door.

Reluctantly, Rika unfolded herself and stepped out, afraid to ask what might be wrong. She followed Dr. Godfrey into a treatment room where Syd was working on a hissing grey-and-black tabby.

"There now, Spider, you're fine. All wrapped and ready to go," Syd said, lifting the irritated cat and smoothly tucking him in a small crate on the table. She looked at them, her brow furrowed. "What's up? You look worried, Uncle Alistair."

"I been readin' the latest CVA Bulletin, catchin' up," he grumbled, a sour look on his weathered face. "There's an article on the spread of certain exotic diseases. From Asia and Africa, imported stock comin' in to Europe mostly. Has this Turkish dog been tested for echinococcosis?"

"I'm not sure. I'd have to call the importer. She has all the paperwork, and that passed through Agriculture Canada screening without any trouble."

"Well, he passed through with a heartworm infection, and who knows what else he may be carrying. So, until we know he's not infected, better not have that girl near the dog."

"That girl has a name—Rika van Wijk." Syd faced him with her hands on her hips.

He waved a hand as if to dismiss her. "You don't want Miss Rika or anyone else exposed to that parasite, is all I'm sayin'. Best to order a test to be sure."

"Oh, Uncle, don't get your knickers in a twist. I'll call Mrs. Brewer and ask if that test has been done. If it hasn't, I'm sure she won't mind if we do it. She's as interested as anyone that this dog is healthy and non-contagious."

"Right," he said and left the room muttering to himself.

Syd could see that Rika was both baffled and concerned. "Oh, boy, where to begin. You're probably wondering what this echinococcosis is, right?"

Rika nodded, wordless.

"It's a disease that you find in places like Asia, South America, and Australia, and sometimes here in North America. It's caused by a parasite passed from sheep to dogs and sometimes to humans. It's an odd disease. It doesn't affect sheep, often it doesn't affect dogs, but it can cause serious illness in people, and sometimes death. So you don't want to mess with it if you can help it." Syd had pulled her auburn braid under her chin and fiddled with the bronze clasp that held her hair in place.

Rika found her voice. "So, Vasi might have this echino... this disease?" she heard herself squeaking.

"It's possible, but not likely. Mrs. Brewer told me they bathe all the dogs they bring back from Turkey before they put them on the plane. Bathing is one way to prevent spread of these parasites. You see, the eggs can attach to the outside of the fur, and if you pet a dog that has them and then put your hands in your mouth, you could get the disease that way. I'm pretty sure he doesn't have the disease, or we would have noticed it by now. With all the X-rays we've taken of his insides, we should have seen some sign of it."

She picked up the small crate holding the cat and peered inside.

"Poor Vasi," Rika lamented. "All the stuff that happens to him. It doesn't seem fair."

"No, it doesn't. Oh well, this test is pretty easy. If we need to, we'll take another blood sample and fecal sample and send them to the Atlantic Veterinary Hospital. They're all set up to do these tests."

"That means another needle."

"Vasi's a brave, tough dog. You know, he doesn't even react to needles, and he's handling the heartworm treatment really well this time. Tomorrow is his last day. I'll call Mrs. Brewer right away. Meanwhile, I guess you can wait for your dad out front. Unless you want me to run you back home."

Rika shook her head. "It's okay, he'll be here in about ten minutes anyway." She felt odd spending time alone with Syd, and she had nothing more to say to her anyway.

By the end of the next day, Vasi was pronounced healthy and fit to go home. And, indeed, he had already been tested for the unpronounceable disease.

As soon as he was released from his cage, Rika wrapped her arms around his thick neck. "Vasi, the sheep have missed you. And pretty soon the coyotes were going to figure out you were gone, so let's get back to work!" He wagged his tail in fierce agreement and pulled her all the way to the waiting truck. Back at home, he bounced into the pasture and caused a momentary stampede of sheep. Rika and her father laughed. Willem put his arm around his daughter's shoulders, delighted to see her this happy.

"Oh, by the way, Rika, Mrs. Brewer called when you were out this morning. I forgot to tell you. She has some interesting news for you."

"What?" Rika could not imagine what news that might be.

"It seems she has a puppy back at her kennel—a puppy from that litter you saw this spring. Anyway, she said you could have him if you were interested, and raise him with Vasi. This would be your puppy to buy." He paused and watched her face. "So, is this something you still want to do? Instead of a Border Collie puppy?"

Rika immediately pictured the darling, fluffy white babies. This one was two months older, but still a puppy. She also imagined herself training a collie pup in Syd's obedience class. Rika had stopped attending the classes, however; she'd been avoiding Syd. She probably had enough money for a pup, and she still wanted to have a collie someday, but maybe this was not the right time.

Rika looked up at Vasi making his inspection of the field, sniffing the ground, raising his leg on posts and large tufts of grass. All thoughts of giving him up had long evaporated. She had grown so fond of Vasi, she could not imagine the flock without him. He was now a part of their farm, a member of the family.

But a puppy. Was she ready for another dog? She could raise him with Vasi's help. And now with the lambs weaned, there were two separate flocks, so it was a good time to start another dog. One who could eventually become a helper for Vasi. Why not?

"Yes, Papa. The timing is perfect for a pup, Vasi can help teach him. I think it will work splendidly." She clapped her hands together and looked up at her father. "Should I call Mrs. Brewer?"

"It is your call to make, Rika."

Chapter Nine

The next morning, Syd showed up at Willemrika Farm before Mrs. Brewer arrived with the apprentice guardian. Rika was annoyed that Papa had invited Syd without consulting her first. This was her puppy, not his. She paced up and down the driveway, wishing Syd would go join Papa in the barn. Instead Syd chatted on while they waited, acting, Rika thought, like nothing had changed.

When Mrs. Brewer's truck finally appeared, Rika practically levitated in excitement. The breeder led a large, bouncy pup from the back of the pickup and stopped in front of them.

"Good morning, Dr. Godfrey, Rika. This is Yeti. He's four months old and full of beans! You'll have your hands full with this one. You call me *any time* you have *any* problems or questions about him," she commanded.

Rika was already on her knees hugging the wiggling, white pup, accepting his long-tongued licks with giggles.

"Gracious, he has grown," Syd exclaimed. "Do you know what he weighs?" She reached down to feel his backbone and ribs.

"Oh, about forty-five pounds," Mrs. Brewer estimated.

"Well, at least he isn't overweight and roly-poly like so many people think pups should be," Syd said.

"That's right. I lecture all our buyers not to overfeed

these giant puppies. They get joint problems when they grow too fast, as you know." She paused to watch Rika rolling on the ground with the delighted, exuberant pup. "You do remember what I said about feeding him, don't you, Rika?"

"Yes, Mrs. Brewer," the girl replied and stood up while the pup tugged at her pant leg. "What does *Yeti* mean? Is it like the Abominable Snowman?"

"Yes, it can be that, but in Turkish it means 'power'." She shook her head. "This big little fellow could be both."

"Why did you get him back?" Syd asked.

"The first owner suddenly decided to sell all his sheep and keep only cattle. He figured he didn't need the pup after all. I took him back, of course, then I tried him with some of our older ewes to test his reaction. Well, he sure minded his p's and q's around them, but those tough old girls are used to these pups. I don't know how he'll do with your sheep, Rika. You'd better watch him carefully for a while," she cautioned. "Probably a long while."

"Won't Vasi keep him in line if he misbehaves?" Rika laughed as Yeti latched onto her sneaker laces.

"Maybe he will, maybe he won't. We won't know until you put them together. Just remember everything I told you about raising puppies. You can't really trust them until they're over a year, and perhaps even older than two years. The boys especially take an *impossibly* long time to mature. Just like people!" She and Syd laughed.

"Uh-oh, here comes a boy now," Syd chuckled as Willem joined them to have a look at the new pup.

He automatically slipped his arm around Syd's waist as he stood close to her. "What is everybody laughing about?" he asked with a generous smile that nearly made his eyes disappear.

"You," Syd answered with a sly look at Mrs. Brewer, who was quietly shaking with mirth.

Rika could not bear to look at them. She buried her burning face in Yeti's soft fur. How could Papa dare to be so intimate in front of Mrs. Brewer? Everyone could see them, even the neighbours across the road if they happened to be outside. She stood up, keeping her back to the adults, and announced, "I'm taking him to the barn to meet Vasi and the sheep, okay?" Without turning around or waiting for a reply, she gently tugged on Yeti's leash, slapped her other hand on her leg to encourage him, and began to trot off. Yeti followed, his entire body and long tail wagging.

Mrs. Brewer marched off after Rika and Yeti and left the amorous couple behind. By now Vasi had spotted the canine newcomer, and his roar from the far end of the pasture was audible all over the farm. It seemed to bounce off the trees and sides of the buildings and echo forever. Little Yeti stopped dead on his big paws. His ears pricked forward and his tail drooped. He gave a little growl followed immediately by a whine.

"Smart puppy, Yeti," Mrs. Brewer praised him. "You recognize the boss, don't you? That's good. Why don't we introduce them away from the sheep, Rika? That way Vasi will have less to be protective about."

The three of them entered the barn where Vasi bristled and growled on the other side of a divider.

"Go ahead and let Vasi in, Rika. I'll hang on to Yeti."

Rika nervously opened the gate and Vasi bounded in, the hair over his shoulders standing nearly straight up so he resembled a charging lion. Rika gasped in alarm. Mrs. Brewer stood confidently while the puppy shrieked in terror, fell to the ground, and rolled over on his back. Vasi stood over him, his body stiff. He growled softly and sniffed the newcomer from one end to the other.

"Oh my goodness, he peed on himself, Mrs. Brewer. Is that normal? Is Yeti all right?" Rika found herself gripping the top of the gate, her eyes wide.

"Perfectly normal, my dear," she assured the girl. "Yeti is submitting to a much older, more powerful member of his canine clan. If he didn't, Vasi would have a reason to attack him. That's how order is kept in packs of wolves and dogs. If you show submissive behaviour to the leader and elders in a group, they will leave you alone and you won't get hurt. If you don't submit when the leader thinks you should, you could get attacked and even killed. It sounds brutal, but that's how it works. When we humans interfere with this order, we create more problems for the dogs we're trying to help out. They generally settle things with a minimum of fuss if we let them."

Yeti had turned back over to lie on his belly. When he raised a paw and tapped the older dog's muzzle, Vasi snarled and grabbed him by the head. The puppy screamed but remained still. Rika felt her knees knocking together, while Mrs. Brewer did nothing. Vasi released his grip, and to Rika's amazement, there was no sign of blood, only slobber. The puppy whimpered, then began to thump his tail and lick Vasi's muzzle. Vasi seemed disgusted and backed away. He lifted his leg against a post then stood at the gate, panting and looking up at Rika.

"Well, that's over," Mrs. Brewer remarked. "He's ready to resume duties now he knows little Yeti is no threat. The next challenge is to see what happens when Yeti goes into the pasture with Vasi's sheep."

Rika could feel herself exhaling a lot of air. She was thankful that Mrs. Brewer was overseeing this introduction. Her hands shook as she opened the gate so Vasi could return to the pasture. She felt a firm hand on her shoulder and turned to see Mrs. Brewer standing next to her, a tender expression on her face.

"My dear, you must remember that these dogs are in many ways similar to wild animals. More similar than many other breeds of dogs. They have their own laws of behaviour. We cannot change thousands of years of patterns that are etched in their genes, so if we want to live with them, or have them work for us, we must accept who they are. If you cannot live with their occasional violence in the name of survival, you should not have these dogs."

Rika swallowed and tried to comprehend what Mrs. Brewer was telling her. She had heard nearly the same lecture in one of Syd's dog-training classes. It hadn't meant too much to her then. Now, suddenly, the light went on. "Survival of the fittest. We learned about that in school. Darwin discovered it," she murmured.

"Well, he proposed the theory of natural selection," Mrs. Brewer said. "But that's the right idea. You're a bright girl, Rika. I know you understand the concept. The hard part is the emotions. We get attached to our dogs, and our sheep, and other animals in our lives. It's so hard to see them quarrelling and sometimes hurting each other." She paused. "You don't have any brothers or sisters, do you?"

"No, but my friend Liz has seven, so I know what you're talking about. And I've seen the rams butting heads. It's really scary, especially when they crack those horns together. You think they're going to break their necks, but they don't, and after a while they settle down and get along. It's just during breeding season they get so mean to each other."

"Aggressive," Mrs. Brewer stated. "Hormones do that to animals. All hell breaks loose. Same with the dogs. We need to keep Vasi intact, since we'll be using him as a stud dog, but you may want to get Yeti neutered before his hormones really kick in. That should ease tensions a bit when Yeti gets older and Vasi starts to feel threatened by him. Vasi needs to be top dog, even when Yeti is larger in size. And Yeti will be a big dog when he's full-grown. So, shall we put him in the pasture?" She grinned at Rika as if they were conspiring together. "Let the games begin!"

Rika opened the gate again allowing Yeti to pass through. He was obviously curious about the sheep, yet still cautious about the big growly dog who had flattened him. With nose to the ground, he sniffed all the small mounds of manure and nibbled on a few.

"Yuck!" Rika wrinkled her nose and scrunched her mouth.

"I know. Puppies can be gross. That's why I don't let puppies kiss me without brushing their teeth first," Mrs. Brewer chortled.

They followed at a distance while Yeti continued to pad around the pasture, getting closer and closer to the flock at the far end. Vasi was lying down where he could watch both the flock and the new pup, and he did not seem perturbed. Rika heard Nosy's unmistakable baa. The ewe came running out of the flock when she noticed that Rika was in the pasture, but her dash was cut short when she realized there was a new dog in her path. She reared up slightly, then stomped both front feet and lowered her head. Yeti recognized the threat and leaned way back until he was nearly down. Nosy stomped again. By now Grumpy was behind her, also stomping feet. Yeti lay down completely and watched them, his tail still thumping hopefully. The ewes decided this was close enough for them and both turned around and ran back to the flock. Yeti popped up and looked like he would give chase when both he and Rika were startled by a blasting, "Arrgh!" barked out by Mrs. Brewer.

Yeti looked for the source of the sound, his ears back and tail down. "That was a correction, to stop him from chasing the ewes. Of course, we could have let Vasi discipline him, but there will be other opportunities,"

Mrs. Brewer predicted. Rika looked at Mrs. Brewer with renewed respect. The lady sure knew her dogs. She would definitely be the leader of any pack she was part of.

"Well, I must be off. You call me with any problems, you hear? And don't feel bad if Yeti doesn't work out to be a sheep guardian. Not all of them do. I'll take him back anytime and find just the right spot for him if he doesn't work out here. With a full refund," she added.

"Oh, no, Mrs. Brewer, I'm sure he'll be okay. He's such a beautiful puppy. I'll watch him carefully, don't worry." Rika was thrilled. Her very own pup. She couldn't wait to show him off to Stirling. She could tell this was going to be one intelligent dog!

Chapter Ten

Rika was true to her word. She put Yeti into the pasture with the ewes, and left Vasi with the more vulnerable lambs nearby. Yeti was a lively, determined pup, and she tried her best to keep an eye on him. He soon lost his fear of the ewes, and she caught him making play bow overtures—rump in the air, front legs flat on the ground—to entice the sheep for a romp. When that didn't work, he charged straight at them, delighted when they scattered like balls on a pool table struck by a cue stick. Even Rika's attempts to stop him with a loud, sharp, Mrs. Brewer–style "Arrgh!" did not distract Yeti from his play focus. Meanwhile, Vasi calmly patrolled the pasture with the lambs while they careened around him. Rika often found him sleeping soundly during the day, surrounded by grazing or resting lambs.

She moved Yeti to share the ram's roomy pen next to the barn, where he was unlikely to get into trouble. Samson did not put up with Yeti's antics. The pup quickly learned to stay out of reach of the hefty ram when he swung his huge horned head or kicked out with his hooves. Otherwise, Samson was good-natured and didn't mind Yeti's company. On the other hand, the puppy was bored and soon earned himself a new name: Houdini. This was

Willem's assessment of the puppy who routinely showed up at the house after escaping from Samson's pen. Every time they reinforced the large pen, the pup managed to discover a new escape route.

Yeti's training was not going as smoothly as Rika had hoped. She had grown so fond of the pup that she was determined to keep him no matter what. One evening in early August, after preparing Willem's favourite dish—pork chops with mushroom sauce and roasted rosemary potatoes from their garden—and setting down the bowls of blueberries with cream and maple syrup, she shared her new vision for Yeti's future.

"Papa, I've been thinking. I believe Yeti likes people a lot more than sheep."

Willem nodded his head. "Ya, I believe you are right. But I think this is normal for all puppies. He must learn to be content to live with sheep. It will take time, of course."

"Yes, Papa, but I think he only *ever* wants to be with people. Mrs. Brewer said that not all of them are good sheep guardians. So I think he would be very happy as a house dog, and I could take him to obedience classes. It won't be the same as having a Border Collie, but he is so friendly I think he would love the classes. And it would be fun to train a different kind of dog."

Willem shook his head and smiled. "Ah, Rika. You need to be more patient. Anyway, this dog is too expensive for a pet. And you have not finished paying for him yet. He needs to earn his keep like every other member of this farm. But first we need to find a way to keep him from escaping, no matter where we put him."

"But he always comes to the house when he gets out."

"Now he does, ya, but as he grows older he will want to travel farther. That was one of Mrs. Brewer's conditions for Vasi, remember? Safe fencing. I think this puppy is more work than you counted on, ya?"

Rika's heart sank. She did not believe Yeti would ever want to remain with the sheep, but she did not want to give him up.

The following Saturday, Willem dropped Rika off at the Farmers' Market in Charlottetown while he ran a few errands. She had arranged to meet Liz at the Market, though she was early for their rendezvous. Rika was standing in the line for apple cider when she felt a tap on her shoulder. Turning around, she found herself facing Errol Keir.

"Oh, hello," she said, and felt her face heating up.

"Hi, Rika. Good day for a cold drink, eh?"

"Uh-huh." There was a moment of awkward silence.

"So how is your dog? I heard he was sick."

Later, Rika couldn't remember at what point Errol bought a glass of cider and a chocolate croissant for each of them, nor how they ended up sitting together at one of the picnic tables outside. She did recall that he was working at his uncle's automotive repair shop for the summer, spent weekends at the beach when he could, and that he missed school. If he had to be called a geek, he was the most handsome geek she'd ever known. His dark blue eyes were mesmerizing. He seemed genuinely interested in her life, the sheep, the dogs, and the fact she would be showing three of her sheep at the Provincial Agricultural Exhibition coming up soon. Their intense conversation was interrupted by Liz's sudden appearance.

"Hey, guys! Great day, huh?"

"Hey, Liz!" Errol stood up and looked at his watch. "I've gotta go, actually. It was great running into you today, Rika. I'll try to make it to the sheep show if I can get away. But if I don't, good luck, eh? Break a leg! Or maybe not?"

They laughed as he headed off and Liz slipped into his place on the bench. She winked at Rika, whose face flared red.

"Oh, he is so into you," she giggled, grabbing one of Rika's hands across the table.

"Do you think so?" Rika's heart raced.

"Well, yeah. You two were hunched over the table like you were plotting something."

"We were just talking."

"Uh-huh. Looking into each other's eyes... you two are so cute together, him with his black hair, you with the blond."

"We hardly know each other!"

"Well, that's not what it looks like. I never see him talking to other girls at school. I thought he was shy."

"He's just interested in the farm, the sheep and dogs—"

"And you!"

Rika blushed and shook her head. "I don't think so."

"I bet he bought you the cider, right?"

"Well..."

"Thought so. Hey, I learned something about Syd and an old boyfriend from PEI. My mom used to go to school with his younger sister."

"Oh?"

"Yeah, I think she said his name was Darrel. They were both going to vet college in Ontario before they built the new college here. My mom said they were engaged for a while. Did you know Syd worked at a vet clinic in Ontario for about five years before she came back to PEI?"

"I wonder why they broke up." Rika was intrigued.

"No idea. I think they worked at the same clinic, though."

"Do you think that's why Syd came back here to work for her uncle? She's just working part-time."

"Are you still mad at her for going out with your dad?"

Rika pursed her lips. "I'm not mad. I just don't get why she'd come back here if she had a good job in Ontario. There aren't many vet jobs here. We don't really know much about her."

"All I know is that she's a great teacher and she's really

kind and good with the dogs. They make a great couple, Syd and your dad." Liz paused and squinted at Rika. "Is this about your mom?"

"No! I just don't want my dad to get hurt. What if she's hiding some awful secret?"

"Yeah, you keep saying that. But maybe you just don't want to share your dad."

"That's ridiculous!" Rika jumped up from the bench. "My dad is probably waiting for me already. See you later." She whirled around and practically ran to the parking lot to wait for his truck. How could Liz even suggest such a thing? Her best friend could be so insensitive at times. As soon as she got back home, she would write Elly a letter. Oh, how she wished her cousin was here to talk to. She was sure Elly would understand. This was a family matter, after all.

Chapter Eleven

Rika was busy the next week, preparing for the largest sheep show of the year. The Provincial Agricultural Exhibition was held in Charlottetown during Old Home Week, near the end of August. Many breeds of livestock were shown during the ten days: dairy and beef cattle, draft horses, quarter horses and ponies, rabbits, poultry, pigs, goats, and sheep. Competitors came from all over the Island as well as other provinces like Nova Scotia and New Brunswick. Livestock judges travelled to PEI from all across the country. This year the sheep judge was from Ontario, and Rika had heard that he raised Oxford and horned Dorset sheep, so she was more nervous than usual. Although her horned Dorset flock was probably the best on the Island, a number of fine animals from Nova Scotia were also entered into the competition this year.

The day before the sheep show, Rika set her alarm extra early. She planned to bathe the one ewe and two lambs she was taking to the show, then put coats on them and keep them in a separate, clean stall until they were ready to drive to the Exhibition. She had already mailed in her entry fees and information on the sheep. A reply had been mailed back to her, confirming her entries and giving her three numbered armbands for her to wear, one for each of the sheep.

Before she even reached the barn that morning, Rika knew something was wrong. There in the grey dawn light, Yeti stood inside the lamb pasture, not in the ram pen where he was supposed to be. He watched her approach, wagging his entire body with anticipation.

"Yeti!" she scolded. "How did you get into that pasture? You are so rotten sometimes!" She walked up to the fence and stared down at him on the other side. "Look at you. Your face is as dirty as a duck's puddle!" She thought this description, used often by Liz's grandfather, was especially suitable considering what Yeti liked to wallow in. "Have you been eating poop again?" She found herself chuckling as she walked away from the fence and into the dark barn to switch on the light. Yeti came around the corner and launched himself at the gate separating him from his beloved mistress. "All right, let's see what you've been eating now. It isn't time for breakfast yet."

She opened the gate for a closer look then put her hand to her mouth. "Yeti, are you hurt?" His muzzle was bright red, not the murky rust brown of Island clay or raisin brown of sheep manure. She felt carefully all over his face but could find no injuries. She then noticed red blotches on his front right paw. She checked him over thoroughly while he continued to quiver with joy at all the attention. Still no obvious scratches or cuts anywhere.

Rika wondered if he'd been fighting with Vasi. She stepped outside and called Vasi's name. She watched as the lambs came running to the barn, with Vasi following behind. He trotted up to Rika, grumbling at Yeti as he passed by him. Vasi stood still while she checked him over for signs of battle, but there was nothing wrong with him, either. Yeti tried to get closer to her, but Vasi growled and snapped at the pup, who jumped out of reach. Then Rika's heart skipped a beat.

She walked among the lambs to see if any of them were

injured, but they all looked fine. She counted them and then counted them a second time. One was missing. She ran to where she kept a large flashlight plugged in, grabbed it, then raced into the lamb pasture, breathing hard.

"Heather, lambie, where are you?" she called for one of her show lambs. It was not long before she found Heather lying on the ground at the far end of the pasture. She was alive, but both of her rear legs were ripped and bloody. The lamb only raised her head slightly when she heard Rika speak.

"Oh, Heather, my poor baby, I'm so sorry," she sobbed, tears streaming down her face. Rika felt a shove from behind and she nearly tumbled on top of the lamb. Yeti's face appeared in the beam of light. He licked Heather's face, then sniffed at her ravaged legs.

"You did this, didn't you?" she shrieked at him, and before she realized what she was doing, she struck him with the flashlight. Yeti yelped and leapt backward, then ran off a few feet. He cowered on the ground, his tail still thumping, his ears back. "What am I going to *do* with you? You are impossible! Why Heather? Where was Vasi? Why do these things happen to me? Damn it!" She was sick to her stomach and confused.

She knew she had to take care of Heather quickly or she might not survive. Where many sick or injured livestock would rally, a sheep would often give up and die. Rika also knew she needed to put Yeti somewhere he couldn't do any more damage. She had never raised a hand against him before, and she felt ashamed. Her mother would have been disappointed in her. Yet Rika thought she might do it again if Yeti hurt another lamb. She tried to swallow her anger, afraid that he would sense it and lose his trust in her, if he hadn't already.

"Come on, Yeti," she sniffled, struggling to keep her voice normal. "Let's go back to the barn and get some breakfast." He stood up tentatively, but then moved toward her, his head and tail down as he followed her back to the barn. Once inside, she put him in a far stall and clipped his collar to an eight-foot chain attached to the back wall. As she closed the door to the pen, he began to bark in protest, high-pitched yelps that gave Rika goose bumps. She ignored him and decided she would need her father's help to bring Heather from the field into the barn. Heather weighed nearly a hundred pounds, and Rika could not lift her by herself.

It was nearly noon by the time Heather's injuries had been tended to and all the usual farm chores were done. Willem sat at the kitchen table sipping his coffee and regarded his glum daughter.

"So, Rika, what are you thinking?" he asked.

"I'm thinking what a big failure I am," she replied honestly. Tears glistened at the corners of her eyes.

"And I am thinking you are too hard on yourself. What will you do next?"

"I don't know, Papa. What do you think I should do?" She looked at him with a pleading expression.

"These are your sheep and your dogs, Rika. I cannot make these decisions for you. But let us look at the choices." He raised his left hand then pointed to his thumb. "First, you can continue on as before, but you need to make very certain Houdini cannot get to the lambs. Second, you can return him to Mrs. Brewer, who has been very kind to us, and understanding. Third, there may be something else you can do to train that puppy not to be so rough. You know, he could easily have killed all the lambs if he wanted to. He was just playing with his sharp teeth."

Rika groaned, remembering the ragged wounds on Heather's legs. "I thought Vasi would stop him."

"Vasi probably did not hear what was happening at the

far end of the pasture. Do not blame him."

"I'm just trying to figure it all out. I feel like a failure. I'll call Mrs. Brewer and talk to her. She can decide."

"Rika, that is not fair to Mrs. Brewer. Before you call her, you should know what you want to do. Okay? And before you make a quick decision, perhaps you should just sit on it for a day. Maybe wait until after the show."

"Yeah, okay. But I'm not sure I want to go to the show anymore."

Willem gave her a stern look. "Now I *am* going to give you some advice, Rika. You made a commitment. You still have two fine sheep and a good chance to win. Everything is prepared—I have already loaded the stock panels on the truck. And other people are counting on you to give those competitors from away a run for their money."

Rika sighed. She stood up from the table. "I guess I'll go bathe and clip the sheep, then," she said, and went outside.

Chapter Twelve

August 20 couldn't have been a more perfect day, weather-wise. As the sun rose over the red-and-green Island, it warmed the cool ground and created a short-lived mist. A gentle breeze blew in from the north shore and kept the temperature from climbing too high. At the Exhibition grounds, happy people wandered between booths that offered chances to win prizes and others that sold pink and yellow cotton candy, or hot dogs and barbecued ribs. Children squealed and screamed on the Ferris wheel and rollercoasters; crowds cheered as horses raced around the long oval track, kicking up clods of dirt behind them.

Inside the livestock barn, all that could be heard was a discordant opera of bawling sheep and bleating goats. High cries of lambs were mingled with the lower tones of ewes and the foghorn blasts from rams. Rika stood next to her sheep pen, more relaxed now that she had shown her ewe and lamb. They had done well. Like other winning competitors, Rika displayed her ribbons on the front of her pen. Her lamb, Gretchen, won first in her breed class of horned Dorsets; her ewe, Karina, took second place for mature horned Dorset ewes. Though it was only noon, she was exhausted from the morning's tension and preferred to stay near her sheep rather than wander the fairgrounds like most of the other young exhibitors. Anyway, she still had one more competition to look forward to: the all-breed championship class for ewe lambs.

"Here you are." Liz appeared with two sausages in buns and handed one to Rika. The two girls sat down on a pile of clean cedar shavings and leaned their backs against the pen. Rika launched into her sausage. She hadn't been able to eat breakfast, since her stomach had been in its usual tangle of knots, and this time her father hadn't even argued with her. At least Heather was up on her feet and eating that morning. In fact, the injured lamb acted like nothing was amiss, even though her rear legs looked like hamburger.

Liz swallowed her last mouthful, cleared her throat, and looked directly at Rika, mischief dancing in her eyes. "I don't know if I should tell you who I saw out there."

Rika gave her an exasperated look. "Yes, you should. And you will."

"Errol was on the Ferris wheel," she replied, biting her lower lip.

"So, he likes rides. I've already seen a bunch of kids from school on the grounds," Rika said in a cool voice, but she felt her heart flutter. She frowned, annoyed at her own reaction to hearing Errol's name.

"Well, he had a friend with him—a girl. Real long dark hair. I couldn't tell much about her 'cause the wheel was moving too fast. She was screaming, just like the little kids," she said, laughing.

Rika shrugged, trying to look uninterested, but she was disappointed that Errol had not bothered to stop by like he'd said he would if he could get away. "Someone from school, probably."

"No, I don't think so," Liz added.

"It's a free country," Rika growled.

"You know, Rika, you say that a lot when you're pissed off."

"I'm not pissed off!"

"But you like Errol," Liz argued.

"So? A lot of girls like Errol, and he probably likes a lot of girls. What do you expect from a guy that cute?" Rika stood up, brushing the crumbs from her white jeans and T-shirt.

Over the loudspeaker, they heard the championship lamb class being called to the ring. Rika's heart raced faster. "Already? Okay, Gretchen, you're on again," she said to her lamb, who continued to chew her cud, totally unconcerned.

Liz scrambled to her feet. "Yeah, go kick some butt out there, Rika!" She beamed at her friend.

Rika led the compliant lamb into and through a throng of bodies surrounding the ring. The judge stood at the centre and pointed each of the competitors into a position. First he read their armbands, then he appraised each lamb. In this class, the winners of all the different breed competitions competed against each other. Rika had the winning horned Dorset lamb. Next to her stood a short, chubby boy with close-cropped hair, barely holding on to his leggy, rearing Suffolk lamb. The racehorses of the sheep world, her father liked to say of the modern Suffolks. On her other side was a girl about Rika's age with a Roman-nosed Cheviot lamb. Next to her stood a grey-haired woman with a black-faced, fuzzy-headed Hampshire lamb, large, solid, and calm as a stocky draft horse. At the far end, a tall man hunched over his stunning Lincoln lamb, her soft fleece hanging in short, silky ringlets all over her body. Rika was sure this flashy Shirley Temple would win the grand champion lamb title.

The judge moved from lamb to lamb, stepping back to study them from the front, the side, and the rear, silently comparing each one to the ideal standard for that breed. He placed his experienced hands on each animal, feeling carefully under the fleece along the back and sides. He also palpated the hams on the lambs to get a sense of the width and length of the rear leg muscles. Finally, after what seemed like eons to Rika, he walked back to the centre of the ring and pointed to the chubby boy to bring his Suffolk forward from the group. He next pointed to the owner of the curly Lincoln to stand next to the boy and his Suffolk lamb, selecting the two most elegant lambs of the group. That meant the Suffolk took third place, and second went to the Lincoln lamb. Rika looked up and was stunned to see his finger now pointing to her, motioning her forward.

Afterward she had no recollection of taking her place, first in line. She barely remembered the clapping, or receiving the huge ribbon for her grand champion lamb, or mumbling her appreciation to the judge as she shook hands with him. She was incredulous. She had won first prize overall with her second-best lamb. Back at their pen, still dazed, Rika led Gretchen inside while Liz pounded her back and gave her high fives. A few minutes later, she returned to earth and found her face was sore from grinning.

"Did I kick butt, or what?"

"You kicked a lot of fuzzy butts, girl!" Liz laughed and slapped her friend on the back again.

"Ooh, I've gotta find a restroom then call my dad. Watch my precious, butt-kicking girls for me?" Still laughing, she trotted off.

When Rika returned, Liz was hopping up and down like one of her crazy popping lambs. "Guess what? Maribeth Riggs, that woman who won in your ewe class, you know, the horned-Dorset breeder from Nova Scotia? She wants to talk to you about buying your lambs. Here's her card. You need to find her right away before she leaves," she urged, still bouncing.

"I'm not selling Gretchen, especially not to her!"

"No, no, she knew you wouldn't sell these two sheep. She's interested in any others you have for sale. You told me you had to sell twelve lambs or have them butchered. Here's your chance! Bet she'll pay good money for them!"

Rika smiled. She needed more money to pay for Yeti. *If* she kept him. She still had not made her decision. First, she had some lambs to sell.

"Do you mind if Syd has a look at Heather's legs when she gets here?" Willem asked his daughter. He stuffed papers into a canvas bag at the kitchen table, preparing for an evening meeting he was attending with Syd.

Rika ran hot water into the sink, scowling. She shrugged her shoulders, annoyed that just the mention of Syd's name had changed her mood from sunny to overcast as quickly as a nor'easter storm blowing in off the Atlantic.

"I think it would be a good idea, don't you?" he added.

"Whatever," she mumbled.

"Rika, you have a very bad attitude toward Syd. Why are you acting like this?" Before Rika could answer, they both heard the sound of Syd's truck in the driveway. The engine died, a door slammed shut, and Syd was at the screen door.

"Knock, knock!" she shouted, laughing.

"Come in, Syd," Willem smiled. "You know you don't need to knock, knock."

Syd walked in, but Rika never turned her attention from the sink, now bubbling with dish soap.

"So how did things go at the show, Rika?"

Rika paused a moment, then spoke without turning around. "Pretty good. Got a second place with Karina and grand champion lamb with Gretchen."

Syd whistled. "Awesome!"

"And tell her about the sheep breeder from Nova Scotia

who followed you home." Willem winked at Syd.

Rika turned her head toward Syd. "She wants to buy nine of my lambs, seven ewes and two rams. So now Yeti will be all paid for. *Plus*, I might have enough money left over for a Border Collie pup," she added and looked directly at her father, soap froth dripping from her gloved hands. "Well, enough for at least half the payment."

"Aha!" he said, and clapped his hands together. "That is what you have been plotting. What a clever child." He smiled at Rika. "Fine with me, if you can raise the rest."

She looked at him triumphantly. "I can." She turned back to the sink.

"Well, it has been exciting around here these past few days." Willem now addressed Syd who sat across the plain wooden table from him. "I told you about Heather's mishap yesterday."

Rika rankled on hearing that her father had already discussed this with Syd. Her lips tightened and she scrubbed harder.

"Rika talked to Mrs. Brewer today, who offered to take the pup back, but my stubborn daughter wants to keep working with him. Mrs. Brewer suggested tying a drag to his collar, something small but heavy enough to keep him from running the sheep or escaping. I just wonder about how safe that might be. What do you think, Syd?"

"Hmm." She considered the idea. "What did you have in mind to use for a drag, Rika?"

Bristling, Rika replied, "I thought we could use one of those small tires. We have lots of heavy chain that won't break. It shouldn't be hard to fix up."

"I'd be worried about him getting caught or hanging up on something. You might want to consider using a dog harness that wraps around the chest and ribs. We've seen cases at the clinic where dogs have been strangled in their collars when they fell off a deck. It's a horrible thing to have happen," she warned.

"I'm not stupid!" Rika retorted. "I'll use a much longer chain so even if he goes over or through a fence he'll have plenty of chain on the other side. Give me some credit, for God's sake!"

"Rika!" her father shouted.

But Rika had already ripped off her gloves and stomped out of the kitchen.

"Rika!" he called again just before she slammed her bedroom door shut.

Inside her room, Rika could hear her father's agitated voice. She cracked her door open and listened from the hall.

"Never mind, Willem. She's a teenager. Teenagers get moody. She doesn't like adults interfering with her plans or telling her what to do, that's all."

"Teenagers should not be rude and use profanity. That is not how I raised her," Willem protested.

"Profanity? Really, Willem. You're too old-fashioned," she chided him.

"And you are too generous."

It was quiet for a moment, and Rika shuddered, imagining that they were in each other's arms, or maybe kissing. Ugh.

"Time to leave for the meeting. I will deal with that rebel later."

Rika slipped back inside her room and closed the door softly. She flung herself on her bed and growled into her pillow. She was *not* a moody teenager! But they *were* interfering with her life—with her and Papa's life. Everything had been perfectly fine before Syd came along. Why did she have to spoil it all? Papa didn't need Syd. Rika would have to find a way to convince him. She just wanted everything to be the way it used to be. Was that so much to ask?

Chapter Thirteen

With the end of August, brisk winds from Labrador chilled the air and churned up deep waters off the north shore. Tourists flocked back home to the neighbouring provinces, the US, Japan, and Europe. As the short summer came to an official end, the beginning of a new school year loomed.

On Sunday afternoon of Labour Day Weekend, Liz and Rika paraded up and down the sandy red shores of Cavendish Beach along with dozens of other teenagers and children of all ages. They ran into old friends from school and town, caught up on their summer vacations, and complained about school starting again way too soon. Occasionally, Liz and Rika stopped to watch the volleyball matches along the stretches of beach. It was a perfect day: hot but not humid, just a mild breeze from offshore, a few wispy clouds, and a promise from the forecasters that there would not be a drop of rain all weekend.

This was the happiest Rika had been since she won the grand champion lamb at the Exhibition two weeks earlier. Willem had agreed to do all of Rika's chores for the weekend so she could camp out with Liz's family near the beach. The girls were thrilled. Liz's mother had assured Willem that Rika would be plastered with SPF 45 sunscreen during daylight hours. Rika had a typical farmer's tan, brown neck and arms. Otherwise she was pale from top to toe, her tender skin untouched by solar rays. Liz was only slightly more bronzed.

"Hey, look!" Liz pointed to one of the volleyball teams. The boys sprinting and lunging across the invisible courts sprayed geysers of sand as they stopped and started. "There's our dashing Errol. Look at those biceps! Ooh..." She breathed heavily and poked Rika in the ribs.

"Ouch!" Rika yelped and stepped back. She bumped into a passing boy who spilled his icy drink on her shoulders. Rika squealed in shock while Liz laughed so hard she fell onto the sand. Rika saw her waving to someone and looked up to see Errol grinning and waving back.

Apparently, he was about to serve the ball. "Hey, keep it down!" he shouted, pretending to look serious. "You're ruining my concentration!"

Liz and Rika watched the all-boys teams play until they had finished the match. Errol's team won two out of three hard-fought games. Afterward, several ran off to the water, diving into the waves to cool off. Errol strolled toward the girls, kicking sand in his wake.

"So what did you think?" he asked, dropping his lanky body into the sand across from them.

"You guys think you're hot stuff, don't you?" Liz teased.

"Yeah, we won, didn't we? I'm hot. You must be cooking in those dresses," he suggested, glancing at Rika in the powder-blue gauze dress she wore over her swimsuit.

"We have to cover up so we don't distract the players," Rika said with a little smirk, then blushed. She couldn't believe what had popped out of her mouth.

"Woooh." Errol shook his two hands like he'd just burned them. "I need some refreshment after losing twenty pounds of sweat. Would you ladies care to join me?" He stood up and they did the same. All three walked toward one of the stands that sold slushies and soft drinks.

Liz kicked at the soft sand as they walked, and said casually, "Saw you at the Exhibition on the rides. Who was that you were with? A visiting relative?"

"Yeah, did you notice the resemblance? My cousin Stephanie from Massachusetts. People usually think she's my sister when they see us together."

Rika choked on her drink. First, she was flabbergasted at Liz's boldness to even bring up the subject. And then to suggest a visiting relative was a stroke of cunning. Errol seemed to be telling the truth.

"We saw you win the grand champion ewe lamb, Rika. Congratulations! But when we looked for you later you were already gone. Sorry we missed you, Stephanie wanted to meet you."

As they sipped their fruit slushies and continued to saunter down the beach, Errol brought up the subject of school. "So, Rika, are you taking Mr. Dunphy's class?"

"Yeah. I hear he's the best biology teacher on the Island. I'm actually looking forward to it. How about you?"

"Yeah, should be good. They're using a lot of digitized computer slides for that course. It's a new website, so you can even access them from home if you have a computer. But then, who doesn't these days?"

"That's great! This is going to blow my dad's mind, study-ing course material on the computer," she said. "Now I can argue for Internet. My dad has been resisting for years."

"Oh yeah? You can play the education card, gets 'em every time. So what kind of computer do you have?" Errol asked.

Neither of them noticed that Liz had dropped behind, a little smile on her face. It was obvious to all but Rika that Errol had a crush on her. And as a loyal, helpful friend, Liz wanted to give them some space.

Rika had always liked going to school, though she wouldn't admit it to anyone but Liz. Willem had never seen her so enthused about starting back.

"Rika, how was day one?" he asked when she came home after the first full day of classes. "Tell me about the subjects you are taking this year."

Rika listed them all and even added the names of her teachers.

"And which of your friends are in your classes?"

"Liz and Stirling and Billy, and Carrie."

"Carrie? You never hang around with her, do you?"

"No, not really. But we're friends at school, and sometimes we do projects together." She sipped on a glass of orange juice she had just poured herself.

"Anybody else?" Willem asked.

Rika looked down into her juice and nearly crossed her eyes. "No."

"No boys that you like?" He tried not to smile, but the corners of his lips quivered.

Rika shot a suspicious look at him. "Liz really likes Sam Gallant. But he doesn't seem interested in girls. All he cares about is racehorses. I think he's immature."

"Oh. What I meant to ask is, are there any boys you like just a little better than the others? Better than Stirling?"

"There's lots of boys I like better than him. He's such a braggart. And he doesn't have anything to brag about." She stood up. "I'd better check on Yeti."

Willem could see she wouldn't divulge any romantic secrets to him, if she had any. "Last time I looked, he was sitting in the middle of the pasture. That drag seems to keep him quiet."

"Good," Rika said, and left the kitchen to change into her chore clothes.

When Rika returned to the house, she could hear her father on the phone. As she pulled off her boots he appeared on the porch, his face long and sad. Rika straightened up, alarmed. Her father only had that look when something dreadful had happened.

"That was Syd calling from the hospital," he said. "Her uncle Alistair just had a stroke. He cannot talk yet, but seems to understand what is happening. They are not sure yet how bad it is."

"Oh," said Rika, relieved it wasn't anything worse. But her heart was pounding. "Well, at least we won't have to listen to his grumpy old voice for a while."

"Rika, that is unkind. Underneath that rough surface, Dr. Godfrey is a caring person. He has been Sydney's guardian all these years, and very good to her."

Rika hung her head and mumbled, "Sorry." Tears began to sting her eyes. Why should she be shedding tears because of that old fart? How could she explain to her father about the fear that gripped her heart whenever he had that look of deep sadness? He would only be disappointed and sadder still to know how distressed she became when she was reminded of her mother's passing. Instead, she decided to ask how it was that Dr. Godfrey was Syd's only relative. She had always wondered, but was too shy to ask Syd herself. And when Syd and her father started dating, she'd decided she didn't care.

"You never heard this before?" he asked, surprised.

Rika shook her head.

"Syd was eighteen, just finishing high school, when her parents died. Her father, Dr. Godfrey's younger brother, was a physician in Montague and her mother was a schoolteacher. Grades five to eight, I think. I hear they were both wonderful people, very involved in their community. Anyway, her father had his pilot's license, and her mother had always wanted to learn to fly, so she got a license as well. They were flying to Newfoundland in early June, going to a meeting, and had asked if Syd wanted to come along. But she had a herding-dog trial she did not wish to miss. It was in Nova Scotia, I think, near Truro. Syd said that dog saved her life, although at the time she wished she had been on the plane with her parents when they went down in the ocean. She was an only child and very close to them." Willem paused, his brows furrowed, his eyes grey.

"I think you have an idea of how difficult it must have been for her. Her uncle Alistair became a parent to her, and it was he who got her through the worst of it. She says he used to be very jolly, always smiling and joking. But he changed after his brother died. Still, he made sure Syd finished university, then veterinary college, and was well taken care of." Willem put his arm around Rika's shoulders and squeezed.

"Did they ever find out why the plane went down? Did they find them, Papa?"

"Ya, they found them. It was a windy day, but they never figured out for sure why the plane crashed. Maybe something wrong with the engine. It was eleven years ago."

"She never says anything about her parents," Rika mused.

"No, she does not, unless you ask her about them. It still makes her very sad to think about them. She misses them. She always will."

Yes, thought Rika, like she missed her own mother. But did Papa miss her as much as Rika did? He certainly didn't act like it.

Two weeks later, Maribeth Riggs arrived at Willemrika Farm to deliver a new ram. She had already taken Rika's nine lambs home with her in August and reported they were doing well on her farm in the Annapolis Valley. While making the arrangements for the lambs, Rika had agreed to buy a new ram from Maribeth. This ram would have a different genetic background from the ewe lambs she had kept back for herself. Since Maribeth was planning to be back on the Island in late September, she'd promised to bring him then.

Rika and Willem were pleased with the ram. He was sturdy and strong and had a perfect set of curved horns on his head. "What is his name again?" Rika asked.

Maribeth chuckled. "We registered him as Manchester's Alfred. Manchester is our farm name, as you know. But my daughters have been calling him Alfie. He actually comes when you call him. A lot of personality, this one. Watch your back during breeding season, though."

"Yes, we know. They're gentle as can be all year, then suddenly they turn sneaky and mean." Rika nodded her head sagely. She had landed on her butt more than once when she had turned her back on a ramped-up ram.

"Syd calls it testosterone poisoning," Willem added, referring to the male hormone that coursed through their veins with extra verve each fall.

Maribeth declined a cup of coffee and muffin, since she had a meeting to attend at the agricultural station. "He should be a good producer for you," she said. "I guarantee all my animals. I'll mail the registration transfer to you next week."

Willem and Rika put Alfie in a pen with their resident ram, Samson. The two rams sniffed each other, pranced around, then proceeded to bash heads and wrestle for the next half hour. They intertwined their necks, pushed, pawed each other with their front legs, backed up, and rammed again. Vasi noticed the commotion from the ewe pasture and came over to watch them, whining each time they cracked their heads together. Once the rams had decided they knew each other well enough, they both lay down a few feet from each other and chewed cud. At that point, Rika leashed Vasi and brought him into their pen. He grumbled a little at the new ram, but Alfie ignored him. Vasi walked stiffly up to Alfie and sniffed him from one end to the other then back again. He then walked to Samson and touched noses with him. Satisfied, he returned to stand next to Rika.

"Does he meet with your approval, Vasi?"

Vasi whipped his tail in circles. "Okay. Back you go. You'll see him in the pasture harassing ewes next month. Just wanted to warn you."

A few nights later Rika was awakened from sound sleep by incessant barking. She lay in bed a while, trying to figure out who was barking and whether it was necessary to get up. It was cold in her bedroom on the second storey of their old farmhouse. Her room had no direct heat, so she used huge piles of wool duvets and quilts on the bed. She remembered Liz telling stories about how her mother's family used to heat bricks in the fireplace just before bedtime. They would wrap the bricks in cloth and place them at the feet of the children in bed. She wished she had a hot brick right now. A clone of herself would be nice, too, to send outside in the wee hours of the night or during raging blizzards.

It was Yeti barking, she finally determined. What was going on now? Rika swung her long legs out from under the toasty quilts. "Damn dog," she muttered to herself, and smiled, thinking how her father would disapprove of such language. Then she rapidly pulled on her clothes to go outside and investigate.

As soon as she opened the back door, a waft of acrid fumes hit her nostrils. "Skunk!" she snorted with disgust, slamming the door shut. She wondered if she should wait until morning to find out who got hit and how bad it was—there wasn't much she could do in the dark. Rika returned to her warm bed but set the alarm for earlier than usual.

When the alarm went off at five-thirty, Rika cursed again. But she got up, pulled on her cold clothes, and went downstairs. She removed a recipe card file and looked under "S." There was the formula she needed: one quart of three per cent hydrogen peroxide, one-quarter cup of baking soda, one teaspoon liquid soap. Guaranteed to remove skunk odour. Who guaranteed it? She couldn't remember if the formula came from Syd or Mrs. Brewer. She found the ingredients and mixed them together, finishing just as Willem appeared in the door of the kitchen.

"What are you baking?" he asked, yawning and stretching his long arms nearly to the ceiling. Like a great, blond orangutan, Rika thought.

"Nothing you'd be interested in, trust me," Rika said with a grimace, pulling on a pair of orange rubber gloves. "Open the door and take a deep breath of the fresh morning."

Willem gave her an odd look and followed her instructions. Immediately, he slammed the door shut again. "Phew! Well, no need for me to contaminate the cows' milk, so you are on your own. Sorry."

"Thanks, Papa, for your support," Rika said, and headed for the door.

"What a girl. Her mother's stubbornness *and* sense of humour. Coffee, I need coffee," he mumbled, shuffling toward the counter.

Rika discovered that Yeti had not been sprayed. Vasi, however, reeked. He was also quite proud of himself. There, in the middle of his pasture, was the evidence: one dead skunk. "Vasi, I don't know who the biggest loser was. Ugh, you stink!" Outside the barn, Rika managed to hose Vasi down, then wash him with the formula. She dried him off with the old towels, but not before he drenched her by shaking his entire body.

She had just enough time for a shower and to change before her school bus arrived. Rika realized too late that she should have used some of the formula on herself. The bus had just started to move off when everyone around her began wrinkling their noses and complaining. Liz verified her fear: Rika stank. How was she going to get through the day? She wanted to shrink inside her clothes and disappear.

At school, she ran to the washroom and scoured her hands with soap. It didn't seem to make any difference. She sat as far away from everyone as she could, and she especially dreaded Biology class, when she normally sat next to Errol. She had been trying so hard to be sophisticated and as cool as any girl from town. How humiliating. But Errol, if he noticed the odour, never said a word about it. To Rika it was the longest day of her life.

The next day and two showers later, Errol caught up to her in the hallway between classes.

"Rika!" he called. She turned to face him. Was he going to say something now? She almost shook with dread.

"You going to the basketball game Friday night?" he asked.

"B-b-basketball game?"

"Yeah, against the Montague Devils. Think you might want to go? Anyway, if you are, Adam and I are going, so if you like we could meet you there. You and Liz, I mean. And maybe have some nachos or wings after?" He seemed a little uncomfortable, shifting from one foot to the other.

"Adam? You mean Adam Wong?"

"Yeah. You know, Adam from Biology."

"Oh, sure. Okay, I guess. I'll check with Liz, but she'd probably like to go. We'll have to get a ride there and back."

"Oh, right. Well, Adam lives out your way. Maybe his brother could drop you off. We'll figure something out," he said, smiling.

"Okay. I'll talk to you later." She waved to him as he turned away then headed to her next class. Sweet, she thought. Wait till I tell Liz!

Chapter Fourteen

When Rika told her father she wanted to go to a Friday night basketball game at a rival high school twenty kilometres away, she did not think it was necessary to mention that boys were involved. Anyway, it wasn't a real date, just a bunch of friends getting together. Still, he found her request a little unusual; she had not shown much interest in basketball before. The two of them would sometimes watch the start of a game of hockey on TV but rarely the end. Living in the Atlantic time zone made for late-night games, incompatible with the early mornings of dairy farmers. However, with Liz in the equation, he did not ask many questions, just that she be home by ten o'clock. Rika eventually talked him into ten thirty after telling him Liz's mother would give them a ride, surprising herself at how easy it was to make such a bold lie. Well, not exactly a lie, since Liz's mother would drop them off at the game. She just didn't mention that they had other arrangements for a ride home, reasoning that if Papa wasn't so strict with her, she wouldn't have to leave out those details. And it was only a basketball game, after all.

Liz was not as enthusiastic as Rika. Although she loved basketball, she did not know much about Adam Wong except that he was a scrawny, awkward-looking boy who hung out with geeks. Still, she agreed to the plan. That's what best friends did for each other. She also enjoyed the intrigue, since Rika's father didn't know about their plans for after the game and Liz had agreed not to tell her parents, either.

They had a good time at the basketball game, though their school team lost. Even Rika was caught up in the cheering and chants, the rhythmic stamping of feet. She began to understand the appeal of watching a live game, felt the energy of the crowd, the connection between packed bodies on the bleachers. The sequential standing up and sitting, the wave of bodies and flailing arms rippling around the court, made her think of the ghostly amoebas gliding on glass under a microscope in class that morning. Errol had been next to her then, too, peering at his own microscope slides. But now he was wedged in beside her on the bench, their arms and legs touching for nearly two hours, the heat almost too much for her. She was afraid to turn her head, worried their faces would touch, they were so close. Liz was on her other side, often grabbing Rika's arm and screaming as a basket dropped through a hoop, no matter which team made the points. By the time the game was over, Rika's ears were ringing and she was hoarse. She and Liz laughed as they filed outside, still giddy from all the noise and energy.

It was a short walk from the Montague High School gym to Sheri's Café. The group of four found themselves the only outsiders in a stream of cheering, high-spirited Montague students all flowing in the same direction. They managed to slip into the last available booth, the two girls sitting opposite the two boys. While they sipped their Cokes and chomped on curly fries, Rika and Liz discovered that Adam was a natural comedian. He had them hysterical with his jokes and antics for nearly an hour and a half. The girls decided he was kind of cute, and in the washroom Rika suggested that Adam had been paying extra attention to Liz all evening. At a quarter to ten, when their ride, Adam's older brother Jason, failed to show up, Rika's mood began to deflate. She did not want to seem worried about a curfew. That would be so uncool. But at ten fifteen, Rika finally got the courage to ask Adam if he should call his brother.

"Sure," he said, and pulled out his cell phone. "Hmm, his cell isn't on. Curious. So we leave a message." He paused a moment. "Hey, man, we're, like, waiting for you. I'm guessing you're in a compromised situation! Nice. Get your butt over here, pronto! Over and out." He snapped the phone shut and slipped it into this jacket pocket. "Don't worry, ladies. He said he'd be at a school dance in Charlottetown. Mind you, he may have forgotten all about us. He's all about hormones these days." Adam noticed the look on Rika's face. "No, seriously, I'm sure he'll be here soon. He's never forgotten me before," he assured her and immediately launched into another joke. Rika continued to smile and forced herself to laugh. She didn't want to let on that she was worried.

Jason walked into the café at ten forty-five, an hour later than he had agreed to. When Adam pretended to complain, he muttered something about a girl he had to drive home first. Adam grinned and raised his eyebrows at the others as they walked outside.

"Yeah, that was ten o'clock," Adam chimed. "Let's see how steamy the windows are. Any signs of lipstick?" He started to examine the interior of the well-used Honda Accord.

"Get in, you turd!" Jason commanded. "The bus is leaving. All aboard!" He beamed at the rest of them, appearing to be very pleased with himself.

Errol and Liz were dropped off first, then Rika. Adam and Jason lived another two kilometres beyond her farm. "It was nice to get to know you away from school," Adam said as she prepared to jump out of the car. "I can see why Errol has a crush on you." Rika mumbled her thanks and slammed the door.

At that moment, she was not concerned about Errol or Adam, but her own hide. She could see that the light was still on in the living room. Papa was waiting up for her, no doubt, way past his normal bedtime, and he was sure to be annoyed with her. She quietly opened the door, her heart skipping all sorts of beats. She hadn't even started thinking of excuses—she knew her father wouldn't be interested.

"Rika?" he called from the living room. His voice did not sound angry.

Rika walked slowly into the room. "Yes, Papa? I'm really sorry I'm so late," she apologized.

"Ya, you probably are." Willem lowered the paper he had been reading to look straight into Rika's squinting blue eyes. "But not as sorry as I am that you lied to me. I am truly disappointed in you."

"L-lied, Papa?"

"Rika, please do not take me for a fool. I know Mrs. Myers did not drive you home. Who do you think I called when you were late? I try not to worry about you, but I do, and I wanted to know everything was all right. So who drove you home?"

"Jason Wong. He lives not far from here. He's Adam's older brother. We were just at Sheri's Café, he was supposed to pick us up before ten, but he was late!" She finished out of breath.

"I just want to know one thing. Why did you say Mrs. Myers was going to give you a ride home when you never even asked her for a ride?"

Rika considered protesting that she never said who was giving them a ride home, but thought better of it. "Because, Papa," Rika swallowed, "I didn't know if you'd allow me to go out if you knew someone else was giving us a ride home. Someone you didn't know."

"And did you know this person? Is there something bad about him that I would not like?"

"No, I never met him before."

"So you were willing to drive around with an older boy, a stranger?" Now Willem looked alarmed.

"No, Papa, it's not like that! He's Adam's older brother. Adam is in my science class at school. Adam's a nice guy, so I thought his brother would be okay, too. Jason *is* very nice, Papa—they both are." Rika was indignant. She had done nothing to warrant this interrogation.

"So, is this Adam a boy you like from school? I never heard you mention him before."

"Well, actually, Papa, he's a friend of Errol Keir's. Do you remember Errol, when he came out to the farm with Stirling and his dad and Billy, this summer?"

Willem shook his head.

"Well, they're both in my Biology class, and Errol asked if Liz and I could stay a while after the game and have a Coke with them. And Adam's brother was going to give us a ride home at ten." Willem looked so dejected Rika almost wished he were angry instead. She trembled, feeling like a little girl just caught kicking a kitten.

Willem shook his head sorrowfully. "Rika, why all this lying?"

Rika winced at the harshness of the word, scraping the inside of her brain.

"You could have told me the truth to begin with. Do you think I would mind if you have a Coke with some friends from school?"

"I don't know," she said in a little voice, tears edging out along her cheeks.

"I want you to promise me something, young lady," Willem said, and reached his hand out to her. Rika approached and knelt beside his chair, crying silently.

"I want you to promise you will never lie to me like that. I know there will be times you will not want to tell me things. We all have secrets and personal feelings we do not want to share, and that is okay. What I mean is purposely lying to me. It is so hurtful to be deceived by the person I love most in the world. Will you promise?" Willem massaged Rika's soft hands in his own large, rough ones.

"Yes, Papa, I promise," she whispered.

"Good," he said, and patted her head, shining gold under the reading lamp. "Now I am overdue to see the inside of my eyelids. We both have to get up early." Rika smiled through her tears at his funny expression.

"Where did you hear that saying?" she asked him, sniffling as they walked upstairs, Willem's arm around her shoulder.

"From poor old Alistair Godfrey, bless his soul," Willem answered.

Rika stopped walking. "Is he dead?"

"No, no. He is too tough just yet. I hear from Syd he is slowly learning to walk again, but I hope we do not see him back here—not at work, I mean," he added. "I hope he is sensible enough to know it is time to retire."

Rika's last thoughts before she drifted into dreamland were of the old veterinarian bossing everyone from a wheelchair. She was smiling.

Syd had taken charge of her uncle's veterinary practice during his absence. Although it was not legally in her name, she had to keep it operating or they would lose clients. In fact, she found herself so busy, she advertised for part-time help. She hired a local veterinarian, Alice Murphy, who had graduated the year before from the Veterinary College on Prince Edward Island.

Meanwhile, Alistair Godfrey, who was getting around with the help of a cane, had accepted an invitation for Thanksgiving weekend at the home of an old friend in Charlottetown. When Willem heard this, he suggested to Rika that they ask Syd to join them for the holiday dinner. In previous years, Willem and Rika were usually invited to have a traditional turkey dinner with the Myers family or one of their neighbours. They found Islanders to be exceedingly hospitable to them, especially after Ingrid died.

At first, Rika was conflicted about Syd joining them, but since she'd learned about Syd's family history, her resistance to the relationship had softened somewhat. Though she still regarded Syd with some coolness, she was keen to take charge of such a complicated dinner. On the Saturday before the supper, Rika showed up at home after a visit to the Myers with a large smoked ham.

"What is this?" Willem asked.

"A mega-ham! I thought we'd do ham for a change this Thanksgiving. I got it from the Myers," she explained and plunked the pink meat in the sink.

"Did you pay Mrs. Myers for it?"

"Sort of. We traded lamb chops and leg of lamb. That's okay, isn't it?"

"Sure, why not? Variety is always nice. Remember, Syd is bringing pumpkin pie."

"Yup. We'll have two desserts. I want to try this one recipe I got from Family Studies class."

"Whatever you say—you are in charge," he chuckled. He had no doubt this would be a fabulous feast. For all her tomboyish ways and competence as a farmer, Rika was a marvel in the kitchen.

They had decided to have their big dinner on Sunday. When Willem came inside the house late in the afternoon, the house was filled with the aromas of Rika's cooking.

Before he could say anything, Rika shouted, "Dinner at five! Better get cleaned up."

"Ya, commandant!" he barked back at her and headed for the shower.

At four thirty, Syd arrived carrying a box covered with a white towel. Now the smell of cinnamon and nutmeg competed with the smoked ham, sweet potatoes, and other scents mingling in the air throughout the house. "Just set it there on the table." Rika waved at her.

"What can I help you with?" Syd stood by the kitchen table watching Rika move quickly between the stove and counter and sink.

"Nothing. Everything is under control. You can go into the living room and keep Papa out of my kitchen. He just gets in the way," she said firmly. With a pang, she remembered her mother saying the same thing to her father. Now it was Rika's kitchen. "Ask him to pour you some wine," she suggested.

Syd laughed and left the busy zone. Rika watched her disappear into the living room and could imagine the picture she created for Willem. In her dark green velvet dress, her russet hair braided and piled on her head, her pale skin, her delicate face and neck, Syd resembled a fragile china doll. Clad in dark blue coveralls, hair stuffed under a ball cap, this same person castrated bulls, set broken bones on dogs, and cut open and stitched up animals every day. Some doll.

Rika heard their voices from the living room where they drank their wine and nibbled on the crackers, apple slices, and cheese she had left out for them. They shouted compliments on the mouth-watering aromas; they commented loudly on the beautifully set dining room table and the walls decorated with gold, orange, and red leaves.

A few minutes before five o'clock, Rika began carrying in the platters of food. Again, she declined offers of help—this was *her* show. They all sat around the oval table covered with lace-edged, cream-coloured linen: a tablecloth brought over from Holland, made by her mother as a teenager. They had not used it since her mother had died, and Rika hoped her father wouldn't mind. She wondered if he even noticed.

Willem sat at one end of the richly laden table, Rika on his left and Syd on his right. They all bowed their heads as Willem said grace. "Thank you, good Lord, for this bountiful feast laid before us today. We stop to remember the good fortunes you have blessed us with. Our health, so we can continue to work and provide for ourselves and our loved ones. And our wealth, in the form of love within our family and for the good friends you have seen fit to send our way. Thank you for all this. Amen." They all looked up at once. Both Rika and Syd watched Willem and each other out of the corners of their eyes. He looked from one to the other.

"A toast," he proposed and lifted his water glass. Syd and Rika did the same. "To good friendships!" Syd smiled and sipped her water. Rika drank and observed the two adults from under her lowered lids.

They ate and ate. The ham was perfect, as were the mashed potatoes, baked sweet potatoes, steamed broccoli covered with almonds in butter, and lima beans in cream sauce. Syd asked Rika about school and they talked about what she was learning in her favourite class, Biology. They discussed how Yeti was still too rambunctious to be left with the lambs and ewes and how well Vasi was doing.

Finally, Syd put down her fork. "If Uncle Alistair was here, do you know what he'd say?" Willem and Rika shook their heads. "I'm stuffed to the guppers!"

Willem laughed. "Ya, that sounds like something he would say. He says a lot of things I do not understand.

His English is like a different language."

"It is—it's PEIslandese!" Syd laughed.

Rika stood up and reached for her father's plate. "Anybody ready for dessert yet?"

"I do not mind waiting a few minutes. I am stuffed to the guppers, too. What about you, Syd?"

"I definitely have to wait. And maybe now is a good time to make my announcement," she gave them a mysterious look, her eyes dancing.

Rika nearly dropped the plate she was holding. Announcement? she thought. Oh no, they're going to get married. She sat back down in her chair, still gripping the plate.

Syd pushed her own plate out of the way and folded her hands in front of her on the table. "Yes, I have an important announcement. On Friday Uncle Alistair officially and legally sold his veterinary practice to me. He plans to stay on as a consultant, which is fine with me. He knows much more than I do about the business end of things. So, isn't that great news?" Syd's face was nearly split in two with her smile.

Willem reached across the table to squeeze her hands. "That is excellent news! Congratulations, Dr. Godfrey!"

Rika also felt buoyant, and genuinely relieved. "Yeah, that's great news Syd. Is Alice going to stay on working with you?"

"Of course. She's really competent, and up-to-date on all the new techniques. If we build up the practice a little more, I expect to hire her full-time. She'll probably concentrate on the small, companion-animal end of things, and I'll do most of the large-animal stuff. We're hiring another veterinary technician next week. I'm *so* excited! And, I've decided to change the name from Iona Veterinary Clinic to something new."

"Well, will you keep us in suspense?" Willem asked.

"What is the new name?"

Syd giggled and covered her mouth like a little girl. "I don't know yet. I wanted to ask you both about that. Any ideas? Rika, you have a great imagination. Maybe you can help me choose a new name?" She smiled warmly at Rika.

Rika nodded her head. "Sure, I'll have to think about it." All she could think about right then was that Syd and her father weren't getting married. And what about Papa's toast? "To good friendships," he'd said. Maybe they *were* just good friends after all, nothing more. Now Syd had her own clinic and a full-time job, she was an independent businesswoman.

"Well," she declared, jumping up, "you guys might be stuffed to the gills—er, guppers—but I'm ready for some of that pumpkin pie!"

"Didn't you make a pie as well, Rika?" Willem reminded her. "A pecan pie?"

"Oh sure, you can have some of that, if you like. I want to try some of Syd's pie."

"Let's have both," Syd suggested.

"Okay, let's do that," Rika agreed and she marched into the kitchen. "Yes!" she said under her breath. "Yes!"

Chapter Fifteen

That there was no marriage on the horizon was the best news Rika was to have for a while. Early November was the start of breeding season on Willemrika Farm. This meant that lambs would be born in April, a much more pleasant arrival than during the icy months of February or March. When Rika put their veteran ram, Samson, in with the mature ewe flock, he ran from ewe to ewe, sniffing them up and down. Most of the ewes were not impressed, and some appeared to show disgust. One or two stood still while he sniffed, their tails wagging a welcome. He would raise his head up to the heavens and curl back his upper lip like he was trying to catch raindrops. Vasi watched this procedure with some interest, but he had seen it all before. He conserved his energy for dusk, night, and dawn, when woodland creatures seemed to be most active. Then he was on serious, nonstop patrol.

In another pasture and out of sight of Samson and his girls, Rika introduced the new ram, Alfie, to the eight yearling ewes she'd kept from last year's crop. Like Adam's brother Jason, she figured young Alfie was all about hormones. In the ram's case, those tiny but potent molecules would totally rule his life over the next few months. He bucked and pranced from ewe to frightened ewe and was rejected by each one in turn. None of them happened to be in heat at that moment, but this did not dampen Alfie's enthusiastic overtures of courtship.

In the adjacent pasture, Yeti watched the antics and became hysterical himself, barking at a high pitch. Rika walked over to calm him down. "You really want to go in there and help Alfie chase those girls, don't you? Maybe you have an identity problem. You definitely have some kind of problem, little buddy. I wish you could watch Vasi and learn from him." She sighed and hugged the huge puppy. He was nearly nine months old and already taller and heavier than Vasi. Yeti was a stunning specimen of the breed, with his jet-black nose, chocolate-syrup-coloured eyes, and flowing, snow-white coat. His paws were still too large for his body, which meant he had a lot of growing to do yet. Mrs. Brewer was right: Yeti would be a giant when he was finished expanding into his genes.

Yeti was in full adolescent mode, and still he could not be trusted with the sheep unless he was slowed down by a drag. She wondered if he would take the full two years to settle and become calm like Vasi. Or maybe three years. Or maybe never.

The question of Yeti's future was settled a week later. When Rika came home from school that day, she found a note from her father on the kitchen table. "Rika, come see me in the barn when you get home," it read. Rika's heart sank. Her father never left her messages like that unless it was serious.

Willem was repairing one of the milking machines in the dairy when Rika found him. "Ah, Rika," he began. "We must discuss that pup of yours. He got into more mischief today."

"What did he do?" she moaned. "Are the sheep okay?"

"Oh ya, the sheep are fine. He was in the barn pen alone for his usual rest time without the drag, but he got out sometime this morning. He must have visited every dog within ten kilometres by the time I got a call from David Reid. He found the pup chasing his purebred Angus calves. We are lucky he did not shoot the pup—he would have been within the law. But he knows Mrs. Brewer, so he called her first, and she gave him our number."

Rika sat on the edge of a bench, her hands on her cheeks, feeling lower and more soiled than the earthworms in their compost bin.

"And Mrs. Brewer called me later to learn if we got the pup back. I think she would like a call from you," he suggested and said no more.

Rika dropped her eyes to the floor. It was clear to her now that Yeti was not happy living the way he was. She shuddered to think he might have been hit by a car, or shot by someone less understanding than Mr. Reid. She knew Mr. Reid's son, Chris, who was a year behind her at school. They were an animal-loving family and had numerous pets, including a Vietnamese pot-bellied pig named Hamlet. "Okay," she said more to herself than her father. "I know what I have to do."

"Rika, remember what Mrs. Brewer said from the beginning," he said gently. "This pup may not be cut out to be a sheep guardian. Not all of them are like Vasi. You cannot blame yourself for this—everyone knows you have worked very hard with that pup."

Rika nodded, then returned to the house. She did not want to see Yeti before she made the call.

Mrs. Brewer was expecting it, as her father had predicted. In fact, she told Rika in a bubbly voice that she already had a rural companion home in Nova Scotia for the people-loving pup if she was willing to let him go. She made it sound like she was sending Yeti off to summer camp and wasn't this going to be fun. She did not act disappointed at all, almost like she'd known Rika would fail. Mrs. Brewer also said she would refund Rika's money unless she wanted to wait for another puppy next spring. Rika said she would think about the offer, but she had made up her mind about Yeti. He had to go.

Rika forced herself to say good-bye to the big pup, hiccupping as she cried. He thumped his tail and licked her wet, salty face. "You'll be much happier with people who will let you inside the house to be with them all the time. Papa won't let me keep you as a pet. It's not fair! I know you love me as much as I love you," she wailed into his fur.

After a while, she dried her face and left him without looking back. She asked her father if he would bring Yeti out for Mrs. Brewer. She couldn't bear to have this kind and unbearably cheerful woman see her so miserable. The look on his face made it clear he understood how painful this was for her.

Rika was so dejected about losing Yeti that she did not tell Liz until a few days had passed. Rika didn't want to let on that anything in her life had changed. But Errol and other friends also noticed her despondence. She would not talk about Yeti to anyone but Liz, and then only over the phone. The tears came too easily, and she hated the feelings of humiliation and failure that accompanied them.

Less than a week after Yeti had gone, Rika had another unpleasant surprise. She was in the barn tossing hay into the mangers one morning when she saw Vasi trotting up to join the sheep. A small, furry creature bounced along a few feet behind him, and Vasi did not seem to notice. Rika dropped the bale she had been holding.

"What the—?" She squinted her eyes—it was a dog! A small terrier type, with short, wiry grey hair, white whiskers, and stocky little legs. The dog was low enough to the ground to walk easily under the larger dog's belly.

Vasi acted as if he didn't see the little dog. Even the sheep ignored him, although they were busy stuffing hay into their mouths. Rika opened the gate to get a better look at the canine trespasser.

She stooped down and the little dog ran to her, panting and waving his long tail over his back. He had a collar on, so he was somebody's pet. Or was it a she? Rika checked out the dog's back end and discovered that it was a neutered male.

"Well!" She straightened up and put her hands on her hips. "Vasi, you've let me down. You're not supposed to let strange dogs into the pasture with the sheep. What are we going to do with you?" She was truly baffled and more than a little disappointed. Rika leaned down again and found a tag with a phone number on the collar. "Okay, little guy, field trip is over. Come with me." She clipped a leash to his collar and he followed her with mincing hops all the way to the house. Rika tied the fuzzy mutt to a porch rail and called the number on his tag. His relieved owners, who lived two roads east of their farm and nearly two kilometres away, arrived within fifteen minutes to pick up Harry. Harry was also overjoyed to see them.

The following Saturday, Stirling and his father paid a visit to Willemrika Farm. While the two men were having coffee in the kitchen and looking over fliers with the latest milking machine technology, Stirling sought out Rika at the barn.

"Hey, Rika!" he shouted. "What ya doin'?"

"I'm reloading the ram harnesses with new marking crayons," she answered. The rams each wore a leather harness with bright oily crayons in a pouch on their chests. When a ram jumped on a ewe to breed her, he left a smear of crayon on her rump, so that Rika knew when each ewe was bred and on what date she should lamb about five months later.

"I heard Harry the mutt outsmarted that guard dog of yours!"

"What are you talking about?" she snapped at him.

"Well, I thought these Akbashes were supposed to keep other dogs away from their sheep. So why did he let Harry get into the pasture?" He smirked at her, leaning against a post. "I heard all about it from Gerry Willis."

Rika was having some difficulty pushing the new crayon into its holder. She stopped and scowled at Stirling. Why was he being such a jerk? "Harry wasn't a threat to the sheep, that's why. Vasi wouldn't let a bigger dog in, or a coyote," she huffed. In a conversation with Mrs. Brewer about the incident, Rika had been assured there was nothing to worry about.

"Oh yeah? How do you *really* know? Have you ever tested him?"

"You can't test guard dogs like you test herding collies. There are no field trials for protecting sheep," she exclaimed. "Wait, I know! Why don't you get a coyote and we'll throw it in the pasture with Vasi and then see what happens. No, no, never mind, I couldn't stomach that. Poor coyote would end up as pasture pizza, too gross." She made a face at Stirling and finally shoved the crayon into place.

"I don't care what you say, I don't think your dog is so tough. He's a pussycat." Stirling turned and left the barn.

Rika finished strapping the harnesses on the rams, fuming the whole while, then walked back to the house. Stirling stood outside, leaning on the porch. When he saw her approaching, he wordlessly pointed across the road where Danny Boy, the Malamute, was sniffing around. The dog crossed the road and started down the driveway toward her house.

"Why don't you get your brave guardian so he can chase off that big dog?" he called out to her. "He kind of looks like a big hairy coyote. Or are you afraid he'll just want to play?" he laughed.

Rika seethed, "Fine! I'll show you!" She whirled around and ran back to the barn, called Vasi, and snapped a leash to his collar. Vasi picked up on Rika's agitation and began to prance with excitement. Rika ran back toward the house with Vasi bounding next to her at the end of a ten-foot leather lead. By this time, Danny Boy was nearly at the house, still sniffing his way from bush to bush, where various stray cats had marked their turf. He did not notice the girl and dog trotting toward him. Vasi, however, spotted him right away. He appeared to double in size as all the hair on his back and neck rose to attention. Rearing up like a stallion, he lunged at Danny Boy with a low growl. The force of his hundred pounds jerked savagely on Rika's arm at the end of the leash.

"Vasi!" she yelled, but she could not stop his charge. His momentum kept him moving forward as Rika tried to haul back with all her strength, both hands gripping the leash. She found herself slipping along the gravel driveway, pulled behind the charging white fury. Danny Boy had now seen the angry dog. His head up, he paused for a moment, then spun around and bounded away.

"Vasi, stop!" Rika commanded, still pulling as hard as she could against the dog straining against the leash. Danny Boy was nearly at the end of the driveway, still running. Suddenly Vasi lunged forward again, then leapt into the air, throwing Rika off balance. She tripped and skidded on the ground with her hands, losing her grip on the leash. Vasi was free!

"No! Vasi, come!" she yelled, rolling on the ground and scrambling back to her feet, her hands bleeding. "Vasi, come!" she screamed as he disappeared around the hedges onto the road in front of their house. Rika sprinted to the end of the long driveway and saw the two dogs on the other side of the road, with Danny Boy still in front and Vasi closing the gap in determined pursuit. As the Malamute neared his home, he veered left and crossed the road again. Vasi followed him, close behind. Danny Boy zigzagged again then ran behind a house, where Rika lost sight of them. She heard a yelp and ferocious growling.

Her legs were numb, but she ran anyway, the adrenalin pushing her forward. As she neared the house she could hear the horrible sounds of the dogfight. Then there was a pause and Danny Boy reappeared around the corner. He was on the run again, with Vasi close behind.

"Vasi!" Rika screamed at him again. He ignored her and continued to run after his quarry. Danny Boy crossed the road again, just in front of Rika. At the edge of her vision, she saw a truck approaching from the left.

"Vasi, stay!" she yelled. But the big white dog could not acknowledge her. Thousands of years of genetic tuning dictated that he must destroy the intruder. He had to get the trespassing dog, no matter what. He ran into the road just as the truck hurtled by. The truck caught him in mid-stride and flung him several feet ahead on the pavement. Then, before the driver could swerve, the right tires of the truck ran over the front end of the white dog who lay limp and crushed in the middle of the road.

Rika heard someone screaming and then she faded to nothing.

Chapter Sixteen

Rika sensed the light filtering through her closed eyelids, but she did not want to open her eyes. What time was it? Why did her hands burn? She cracked her lids open and saw sunlight streaming through her bedroom window. Why was she lying on top of her bed, fully dressed, in the middle of the day? She lifted her aching hands in front of her face. They were wrapped in white bandages, but she could not remember hurting them. Then a scene flashed across the screen of her mind, a white body flying through the air, landing hard.

"No, no, no," she moaned. Then louder, "No, no, no! *Noooo!*" She turned on her stomach and buried her face in the pillow. She began to breathe in and in and in— she couldn't stop and she couldn't breathe out. "Arrh!" Her breath finally rushed out and her stomach muscles wrenched. She leaned over the bed and began to vomit what little was in her stomach. She heaved and heaved until there was nothing but air left to expel.

The bedroom door opened and someone walked in. "Go away!" she screamed. "Get out of here!"

"Rika, it is Papa." He touched her shoulder gently.

Rika struck his arm so hard it flew up to his face. "Get out!" she yelled again. Willem stepped back a little, his face pained. He put his hands out then gently, but firmly, held Rika by the shoulders and looked closely into her face.

"Rika, you are in shock. Rika, listen to me," he pleaded.

"No, go away! I don't want anybody! Go to hell!" she screamed and began pounding his chest with her fists, not feeling the pain. Willem grabbed her wrists to still them.

"Okay, Rika, I will leave you for a while. You need more time, more rest." He let go of her hands and she recoiled, curling up into a ball on her side. She reached for a pillow and drew it over her head. She heard the door close.

It was dark when Rika opened her eyes again. She wondered how long she had slept. She vaguely remembered Papa coming into her room and she remembered being angry. There was a sour smell in her room and she felt a wave of nausea. Slowly Rika rose to her feet, her entire body aching, her head pounding, and wobbled out of her room into the hall. She could see that the lights were on downstairs so she tiptoed to the bathroom. When she emerged again into the hallway she heard voices, and stopped to listen. A woman spoke.

"I know, but she said she'd take care of expenses. Anyway, we're not there yet. First they have to decide if they need to amputate." Syd's voice. Rika heard a groan. Papa.

"Oh my Lord, that poor dog. Would it not be better to have him put to sleep?"

"They didn't think the internal damage was serious. He's one tough dog, Willem. And lucky. As soon as he's stabilized, they can get him into surgery."

"I suppose there is no sense in telling Rika anything until we know more for sure."

"Yeah, they promised to keep us informed. And if I don't hear from them, I'll call. Willem, I have a feeling he's going to pull through."

"I hope you are right, Syd, for Rika's sake. She would never forgive herself. She was already so depressed about

Yeti, now this—and the way she reacted earlier. I know she is in shock, but I worry. She did not even react this way when her mother died. In fact, she hardly reacted at all. She kept it all inside, I think. Of course, she was much younger then. Perhaps she should have seen a therapist, but she was handling it so well. I was the one falling to pieces. Now I worry, I am afraid she might do something drastic." There was a pause. Rika's heart raced and her legs began to buckle as she leaned on the banister.

Willem continued, "I never told her, but one of my uncles committed suicide. It was just after the Second World War, in Holland. He had reported on a Dutch family who was hiding Jews, and the Nazis sent them to concentration camps. The entire family and the refugees. After the war was over, and before we even knew what he had done, he hanged himself. It was a terrible time for our family."

"Oh, Willem, those were such terrible times for everyone. But Rika may be overreacting from the shock, and perhaps a sedative wouldn't be such a bad idea right now."

Rika turned quickly and returned to her bedroom. How dare they talk about her like that, like she was crazy or depressed. She'd show them.

The next morning, Willem knocked on her door asking if she wanted some breakfast. Rika's head still ached, and although her stomach growled, she was not interested in eating. She let him make her some weak tea, which she drank in her bedroom. Then she let him change her bandaged hands. Her right hand was particularly badly scraped. Willem gave her a Tylenol for her headache and she went back to sleep. But she was restless, and her old nightmares returned, mixed with scenes of bloody coyotes and bloody sheep. Then it was night again, and she lay wide awake, wondering if sedatives or sleeping pills might be a good idea. Anything to keep her asleep, a deep sleep without the horrible dreams and visions.

The following noon, Rika dressed herself and went downstairs on wobbly legs. She felt a bit fuzzy, but her headache had disappeared, and her hands did not hurt unless she flexed them too much. She made herself a bowl of instant oatmeal with fresh cream and maple syrup drizzled on top. Normally she didn't care for oatmeal, but today it seemed like the only food she could keep down. She was sitting at the kitchen table when her father walked in.

"Ah, you are up. And eating. How do you feel?" he asked with a wide smile and arms open to embrace her. Rika turned her face down toward her bowl.

"I'm fine," she mumbled and scooped up another mouthful.

Willem stopped, then slowly turned to the coffee pot on the counter. He poured himself a cup while Rika continued to play with her spoon in the bowl, scraping the last few globs of oatmeal from the sides.

"That is good, then. Were you able to sleep last night?" he asked as he sat down across from her, gripping his cup with both hands.

Rika considered telling him the truth, but decided that she would not play into the victim game. "Fine, just fine."

"Good," he said, and sipped his coffee. "Ah, forgot the sugar! I am getting absentminded." He reached for the sugar bowl on the table. "We have some good news about Vasi," he said, and looked at Rika, smiling again.

She remained silent and continued to scrape her bowl.

"He had surgery at the Veterinary College and he is recovering nicely. In fact, everyone is amazed at how well he is doing."

Rika stared into her bowl. Was he going to tell her about an amputation? Maybe there wasn't one after all; maybe she had dreamed the conversation he'd had with Syd. But she didn't care. Vasi was not her dog, he never was, and he'd be going back to Mrs. Brewer, anyway.

"What day is it?" she asked, popping her head up to see her father staring at her in surprise.

"Today is Monday," he said.

"So I'm missing school."

"Ya, but that is okay. You need a little time to—"

"I don't need any more time. I told you, I'm fine." With that, Rika rose from the table, stiffening her legs to hide shaky knees. She put her bowl in the sink and returned to her bedroom.

In the following days, Willem continued to give Rika progress reports on Vasi. He told her about the front leg that had to be amputated. He described how with only three legs, Vasi was already able to stand, walk, and even balance on one front and one back leg to urinate.

Once he was well enough, they transported Vasi to Syd's clinic, where old Dr. Godfrey insisted that they offer rehabilitation and recovery services free of charge. The senior veterinarian managed to get himself to the clinic once each day to keep an eye on things. Syd also dropped in to give Rika updates. She said that although Alice Murphy found Uncle Alastair exasperating at times, he seemed especially fond of Vasi and brought him treats every day. Alice had even overheard him having civil conversations with the dog when he didn't think anyone was listening.

Rika sat silent, avoiding eye contact and never commenting on the Vasi reports. What did they expect of her, anyway? None of it mattered, now that she had failed so spectacularly. She couldn't train a puppy, she couldn't even keep a valuable trained dog safe. She made stupid, costly mistakes and she was a liability to her father. She wished they would stop trying so hard to involve her in something she didn't care about anymore. Caring for her sheep had become an onerous chore, and Rika began to think about selling the entire flock. She had to find some way to pay for all the damage she'd caused. It was obvious that she was not fit to care for any creature, and she did not deserve to be her father's partner in the farm. No wonder he'd sought out the company of Sydney. She'd even failed at being a good daughter and company for him. She was totally useless.

One evening after supper as Willem washed the dishes and handed them to Rika to dry, he said, "So, Rika, what do you think about a trip to Holland for Christmas this year?"

Rika did not look up as she wiped a plate and slipped it into a cupboard. "No thanks, Papa, I'd rather not. Any more glasses to do?" she asked, staring at his hands where they soaked in the soapy water.

Willem frowned. "Don't you want to see Elly and Oma? I know they would love to see you. It has been a long time since we were back—"

"I don't feel like travelling right now, okay? Anyway, it costs too much." She glanced up at her father, his mouth still open, his expression confused and worried. "I'm fine, Papa. I don't need a trip." She sighed and shook out the dishtowel. "Are we done with the dishes?"

Willem regarded her a moment longer. "Ya, we are done here." Rika tossed the damp towel over the back of a chair and left the room without looking back.

Chapter Seventeen

On a frosty Saturday afternoon in early December, Rika shuffled around the kitchen, grumbling to herself. How did Papa and Syd ever talk her into making *pepernoten*? Even though she loved the traditional Dutch cookies, she had not been in the mood to bake anything for quite some time. It had started at dinner the night before. Papa was explaining some of their Dutch Christmas traditions to Syd while Rika sat quietly at the table, picking at her food.

"In the Netherlands, we celebrate St. Nicholas on December 6," he began. "In Dutch we call him Sinterklaas."

"And here he's called Santa Claus," Syd said.

"Yes. The original Sinterklaas was a bishop, a kind man who helped poor children and destitute women. Oh, and you might find this an interesting connection. He was born in the fourth century in a town on the Mediterranean coast in Lycia, which was Greek back then but is now part of Turkey. He became the patron saint of sailors, fishermen, repentant thieves, and children. They say he had a habit of secret gift-giving, and that legend became our Sinterklass. Traditionally he is dressed in red medieval bishop's clothing, with a long cloak, sometimes trimmed with fur."

"I think our Santa could use a wardrobe makeover," Syd suggested. "Does Sinterklaas travel in a sleigh pulled by reindeer?"

"No, our Sinterklaas comes by boat from Spain, then he mounts a magnificent white horse and rides over the rooftops of Holland on the night of December 5. He slips down chimneys to deliver toys and cookies and he puts them in the waiting wooden shoes of all the good children."

"And what about the bad children?" Syd asked, laughing.

"Ah, the bad children receive a lump of coal or a switch. And Sinterklaas is accompanied on his travels by one or more mischievous helpers called Zwarte Piet, or Black Peter. Here you have those little elves in green suits. In some Eastern European traditions, they have angels travelling with St. Nicholas."

"What about the food? You must have special food or treats, like fruitcakes or cookies?"

And that was when Willem explained about the meal on December 5: buttery winter turnips and carrots, mashed potatoes mixed with special herbs and laced with leafy green kale, sausages, and three different types of Christmas cookies. Those included the hard, round, acorn-sized cookies flavoured with ginger, cinnamon, and nutmeg, which some people called *pepernoten*, or peppernuts.

Now Rika was staring at the recipe card in her hand. Her mind drifted back in time, and she could picture her mother in the kitchen, her hair tied back in a ponytail. She remembered sitting on a tall stool in the kitchen, watching Mama mixing dough, handing her the spices all lined up on the counter. Her mother would be singing Christmas songs in Dutch, and Rika would hum along. She remembered the flour on her mother's forehead, the hot, steamy kitchen, the spicy aromas from the oven. Then suddenly Mama was gone.

Now here she was, alone, collecting all the ingredients for *pepernoten*. In spite of that unwelcome chore, Rika was happy enough to be by herself in the house. With the wood stove blazing and the oven on, the kitchen windows had fogged over and she could pretend that the outside world did not exist, that she lived alone inside a giant, hollowed-out *pepernoten*. Much more pleasant than Cinderella's pumpkin coach, she mused.

Rika thought back to earlier that morning, the way Syd and Papa had acted when Syd came to pick him up to do some shopping. They were both giggling and silly and downright irritating. Rika no longer cared that they were spending so much time together; she knew she wasn't much fun to be with. A few days before, when Papa finally offered to get Internet service and let her have a home email account, she had just shrugged her shoulders. There was no one she particularly wanted to write to anymore. She almost smiled when she saw his look of disappointment and confusion, and then she got angry. He just didn't get her. Through it all she showed no emotion. What was the point?

Rika had just taken out the last pan of cookies when she heard the truck drive up. She didn't bother looking out the window—it was too steamed up anyway. Then she realized that there were more than two doors slamming shut. She paused to listen. Someone else must have arrived at the same time. Still, she didn't bother to clear off the window to take a peek as she placed the pan on wire racks so the *pepernoten* could cool. But when the outside door opened and she heard several voices all speaking Dutch, her body stiffened and she began to tremble.

The first person through the kitchen door was a tall, stout woman with a round face and short blond hair, a pale blue scarf wound around her neck. She wore a huge dimpled smile in spite of the tears streaming from her squinting eyes. She opened her arms wide and cried, "Rika, my treasure!" as she bore down on the startled girl. Rika found herself backed against the counter, wrapped in a tight embrace.

"Aunt Martina?" she managed to squeak. What the hell? What was going on? Then from beyond her aunt's sobbing shoulders, Rika watched as Oma Wilma, her grandmother, and her cousin Elly entered the kitchen. Rika was unwrapped and gently pushed toward her Oma, who also clasped her, but with less force. The feel of papery skin on her cheek and a smell from the distant past caused a jolt of electricity to pulse through Rika's brain and senses. Although it was Oma kissing her, holding her tight, it was someone else, too. That smell, what was that smell? Not unpleasant, but evoking some uncomfortable feeling that made her stomach stir.

Then there was Elly, standing back with Willem and Syd, her arms crossed, a cautious, curious expression in her heavily made-up eyes, pink glossy lips set in a grimace. This was not the cousin Rika remembered. Elly was just a little shorter than Rika, but she had the same blond hair and complexion. However, where Rika's hair hung straight and limp to her shoulders, Elly's hair was cut short in the back, with long, sweeping bangs that nearly covered her eyes. Rika had never seen Elly wearing makeup before. And there was the stud in her nose, a glittering rhinestone to match the studs in her ears. In her black tights, short black skirt, waist-length leather jacket, and thick-soled boots, Elly looked like she had walked off the cover of a teen fashion magazine. In fact, she could have been mistaken for a twenty-five-year-old model.

What followed was a lot of chatter, translating back and forth for Syd's sake, and comments on how wonderful everyone looked, especially Rika, who remained mute through it all. Martina had grasped Rika by the shoulders and did not seem to want to let go of her.

"And you made *pepernoten*! What a clever girl. Elly would not be caught dead in the kitchen, she has more *important* things to do. You are such a blessing to your father," she gushed. Rika felt her colour rising. She was desperate to break away.

"Huh!" Elly snorted. "Mama, you are a control freak. You don't want me in your kitchen. Tell the truth!" She rolled her eyes then winked at Rika.

Rika finally spoke up, her voice unsteady. "Papa, you never told me. We don't have anything ready for visitors. The rooms—"

"The rooms are ready. You did not even notice, did you? Syd and I were very careful not to arouse your suspicions. We wanted it to be a surprise. I think we succeeded, did we not?" he beamed at her.

"You folks must be exhausted after your long flight over," Syd said to the travellers. "Why don't we show you to your rooms and then perhaps we can have some tea—if you like."

"Ya, that would be lovely. Mama? How do you feel? Do you want to lie down for a little?"

Wilma van Wijk shook her head and frowned at her daughter. "Ya, tea would be very nice. We have done nothing but sit for hours. I am not so decrepit yet, Martina. Perhaps *you* would like to take a nap," she said, pointing her finger at the laughing woman.

Syd led the two older women out of the kitchen to the room they would be sharing. Rika felt she could finally breathe and motioned for Elly to follow her. She assumed her cousin would have the small room next to hers, and her aunt and grandmother would take the large room with two beds at the end of the hall. Those had been the arrangements the last time their Dutch family had visited them, for her mother's funeral. Her mother used to complain about the size of this old farmhouse, but Papa always said it would be perfect for all the visitors they would have. Rika was certain he was disappointed that

124

his family had only visited the one other time when she was five years old, but he never showed it. That was his way—he did not share sadness. That was her way, too.

Once they were in Elly's room, her cousin looked around, hands on hips, then stared at Rika, who stood in the doorway. "Close the door," Elly said, beckoning her inside. Rika did as she was told.

"So, tell me, little cousin. What's the story? You've changed, you look like hell. Is that saintly father of yours working you to death?" Elly grabbed the one chair in the room. She flipped it around then straddled the seat and folded her arms across the back.

Rika's mouth fell open for an instant before she recovered. "So," she said, "you've changed, too, cuz. What's with all the makeup? Can I use some?" she asked, hardly recognizing her own voice. She felt her heart racing, and her chest expanding, like she was holding back a ravenous, caged creature.

"Uh, ya, sure. Right now?" Elly looked surprised.

"Yeah, right now, eh?" She smiled at Elly, who returned her own wary smile.

"You Canadians are odd. But nice."

"Well *you*, cuz, are cool. I think it's time for a Rika makeover. Wait till my hick friends see me!" She laughed when she imagined Stirling's stunned face. For some reason she did not picture Liz or Errol. She only saw Stirling, and she wanted to shock him, to see him squirm.

That night at supper, Rika marched in with Elly and was pleased to see that the table had already been set and that there were at least three cooks in the kitchen bearing platters of food to the dining room. No one remarked on Rika's new made-over look, although Oma's smile turned to a frown at the first sight. Besides the eyeliner, mascara, and light face powder, Rika's nails had been painted a dark blue. In the dim light they appeared black, like Elly's. Rika knew from the raised eyebrows that the adults did not approve of the new look, and that pleased her. In fact, she was delighted, happier than she'd been in weeks. She'd just needed her uber-cool cousin to light the way for her.

On Monday she and Elly were going to get her a new haircut. Something radical, something that would blow their socks off. She could hardly wait. Papa had agreed that she did not need to go to school every day while they had their visitors, but she would have to find some way to keep up. Liz and Errol and a couple of other friends would take good notes for her; she had it all arranged. This was going to be perfect.

Chapter Eighteen

Monday was a slow day at the hair salons, so Rika had no trouble getting an appointment. To her delight, Elly was allowed to drive the rental car into town. Elly, who'd had her licence for over a year already, convinced her uncle that she was a good driver. Her mother did not contradict her this time. However, Martina did not feel her daughter should drive at night, especially in a strange place. Elly just snorted at this comment and said nothing as she reached her hand out for the car keys.

"And watch the roads, young lady," Martina continued. "You are not used to driving on snow."

"There is no snow on the roads, Mama. And it won't snow today, right, Oom Willem?" He nodded his head, smiling broadly at the two girls who were bouncing in their impatience to get away.

Once they were out of sight of the farmhouse, Elly stepped on the gas, laughing as the car surged forward. Rika swallowed and gripped the armrests. She was not comfortable driving during the winter, hadn't been since her mother's death. The last time she had seen her mother, she had sped off into a frigid January night. Rounding an icy curve in the road, she had lost control of the car. It had rolled three times through a ditch and into a field, landing upside down, crushing the life out of her. Rika gritted her teeth as Elly hit 100 kilometres per hour on their country road. In a way, the danger was exhilarating. Anyway, there was no snow or ice, so she kept her peace and her eyes off the speedometer, still gripping the armrests.

By the time they walked into the hair salon in Charlottetown, Rika was in high spirits again. When it actually came time to select a cut, she was uncertain. Although she liked most of the wild, modern styles in the salon magazines, she could not identify with any of the drop-dead gorgeous models posing with the daring hair. Finally, she settled on a cut similar to Elly's but which left her hair a little longer in the back.

"It's going to take a lot of gel and styling to keep it from lying flat," Elly warned.

"No problem," Rika said, although she had never used gel in her life. She was not usually that particular about her appearance, and with chores to do morning and evening, she did not have time to fuss with her hair. Long and straight had always worked for her. From a very early age, she would mimic her mother, who liked to say, "Less is more." Now she found herself studying the stylist's every move so she could reproduce the hairstyle on her own later. By the end of the procedure she was more than pleased with the result, but realized she would have to get up an hour earlier each day to keep it looking like that. At that very moment, she didn't care—she couldn't wait to show it off.

The two girls, looking more like sisters than cousins, found a nearby café to have lunch. It was a Lebanese place that served wraps and falafels and savoury salads. Rika wanted to impress on her cousin that they did have one or two excellent ethnic restaurants in little old Prince Edward Island, even if they weren't as cosmopolitan as the city Elly lived near. Elly did not compliment the food, but she didn't criticize it, either, so Rika felt she had succeeded.

"What about Juliana? Your mother said she was in Antwerp now. How does she like it there?" Rika asked about Elly's sister, who was eight years her senior.

"That lucky bitch," Elly started, while Rika choked on a piece of pita bread. "Imagine being a fashion designer in a prestigious shop in that fabulous city. No one ever sleeps in Antwerp, such fantastic nightlife, you wouldn't believe! But she worked hard to get there, I have to give her that. Mama and Papa didn't think it would ever happen, she was hell on earth when she lived at home. I'm a dream child in comparison." She grinned at Rika. "Hard to believe, ya?"

Rika grinned back. No doubt Aunt Martina had her hands full.

"And what about Syd? Isn't that a man's name?" Elly bit into her falafel, wrinkling her nose.

"Yeah, Sydney can be a man's or a woman's name. Sydney Anne is her full name," Rika mumbled, then took a sip of her tea, avoiding Elly's probing eyes. "She's okay."

"Mm-hmm. Did you know that Mama has been trying to hook up your papa with a widow back home?" she asked. Rika gulped and shook her head. "Ya, her friend Beatrix. She's a pastry chef. Nice lady, I guess, but she has this eight-year-old brat and I wouldn't wish him on anyone. Spoiled! Worse than Oom Dirk's boys, and they are insufferable." She smirked at Rika, who looked down again. What else did Elly know about Papa that she didn't?

"But then, you know what your papa said to Mama?" She paused for effect but did not wait for a reply. "He said that he had a lady friend on Prince Edward Island and that they were as tight as two coats of paint!" She paused again and sipped her coffee. Still Rika said nothing.

"'Two coats of paint.' A strange expression, but at the same time it sounds erotic, don't you think? So, does she spend the night, or does he go to her place?"

Rika spluttered and wiped her mouth. "No! She does not stay over, and he does not go to her place." Her cousin had a lot of nerve.

"How do you know? Are you always with them? Of course not. I think they are serious, in case you've been too busy to notice. Do you think they'll get married?" Elly pushed on.

"I don't know. Papa hasn't discussed it with me, and he would if he ever planned to marry again. Which I don't think he is, but it doesn't matter and I don't care one way or the other!"

"You don't need to get so defensive," Elly said. "I'm only telling you what I heard."

"I'm not defensive!" Rika retorted, then looked at her fingernails. She took a deep breath. "I just don't care, okay?"

"Okay. We having dessert?" Elly asked. "That baklava looks good."

"You go ahead, I'm too full."

"Okay. Listen, I have some good news for you," Elly leaned over the table, tapping her long black nails on the polished wood surface and smiling at Rika.

"Yeah?"

"Mama gave me some extra money to take you shopping. It's an early Christmas present for you. And your birthday, too. Isn't it next weekend you turn fifteen? Don't look so shocked! We're going to get you some new clothes, girl, smarten you up. You have been on that farm way too long. What do you think? Is that good or is that good?" Elly slapped the table with both palms, clanking her silver bracelets.

Rika sat up straight and stared at her cousin. She was serious. "Uh, that's good. That's, uh, excellent." She felt her face thawing a bit, a smile creeping in.

"That's more like it. Feel like dessert now?"

"No, still too full. Maybe I'll take a nibble of yours."

"Fine, but just a nibble," Elly grinned at her then leaned over and pinched Rika's cheek.

"Ow!"

"Just checking to make sure you're still alive. I don't want to go shopping with a dummy. You'll do."

Rika felt light-headed, feverish. It was like a fairy god-mother had flown in from Holland to bless her with riches. She thought she should be delirious with happiness, except some small nagging detail kept tugging at her. Wouldn't it be great if Elly and Aunt Martina, and even Oma, could live nearby, or maybe with her and Papa? Or perhaps she could go back to Holland to live with them. Papa had a lot of good friends, including Syd. He hadn't been paying that much attention to her since Syd came on the scene. Rika would be leaving home eventually, and maybe, without her around, maybe he *would* marry Syd. Then Papa wouldn't be lonely. Yes, that could work out. And so she imagined all sorts of scenarios while they shopped. With Elly's fashion advice, they outfitted her with a couple of stylish tops, one with sparkles, a short skirt, a black jean jacket, and metal-studded boots.

On their way home, Rika suggested a short detour to pick up the school notes Liz had collected for her. But mostly, she wanted feedback on her new look. As she expected, everyone at the Myers' home was amazed by her physical transformation. They stared and stared, all the little ones clustered around her like baby birds waiting to have their gaping beaks filled. The older ones commented on how alike the two girls were. Mrs. Myer insisted that they stay for dinner, although Rika resisted. It was Elly who accepted the invitation with enthusiasm. When Rika gave her a questioning look, Elly whispered that it would be fun. So Rika called home and told her aunt not to wait on them for supper. When Martina protested, Willem assured his sister that the Myers were a short drive away on a quiet country road.

Given how cynical Elly was about most things, Rika was unprepared for her cousin's apparent charm and generous behaviour amid the squabbling children and general din. Liz said barely a word and hardly met Rika's eyes. Afterward, the three girls convened in Liz's bedroom, which was even smaller than Elly's guest room at the van Wijks'. Elly spun around, taking in all the details.

"These bed ruffles are so nice. We have them in Holland, also. But we like stronger colours, you know, like bold reds, or mustards or olive green. And this is nice lacework on your window. Did your mother or grandmother make it?" She rubbed the lace curtain between her fingers, staring at Liz.

Liz turned bright red. "No. Mother bought it. She doesn't have time to do that kind of stuff. You know, with the kids and all—"

"So how do you like Rika's hair?" Elly interrupted. "You never said. Don't you think it's such an improvement on her straight hair? You know, I saw a perfect style that I think would suit you, Louise."

"It's Liz," she said, still red-faced, and turned away from Elly's scrutiny. "Here are the notes, Rika. Errol said the Biology assignment isn't due until next week."

"Okay, thanks, Liz. I'll give you a call later, okay?" Rika said in a near whisper and took the notes from her friend. "We'd better go, Elly. It's already dark and your mama will be worried."

"What? You are also afraid of my driving?" she asked, hands on hips, laughing.

"No, I'm not afraid. Let's go. See you, Liz."

Liz nodded her head. "Uh-huh."

Once they were in the car and heading home, Elly began to laugh. But her voice had an edge when she said, "Rika, my dear, *that* girl is your best friend? This explains a lot. I think you have potential, but you have to watch who you choose as your friends, your confidantes. Not to worry, just stay close to me. There is hope for you. After all, we are related."

Rika remained silent. Seeing Liz's family through Elly's eyes had opened her own. Yet, she was uncomfortable having any bad thoughts about her old friend. Liz was the sweetest girl on earth, the most loyal friend one could ever ask for. Still, she seemed so simple and backward and dull next to Elly.

As soon as they walked in the door, Rika found her aunt and gave her a big hug and thanked her for the new Christmas clothes. Martina beamed at her niece, complimented her new hairdo, and told her to show it off to Willem. When Rika entered the darkened living room where her grandmother and father sat reading by lamplight, Oma's first response was to say, "Elly? Where is Rika?"

Rika laughed. She didn't think she looked anything like her cousin, but in the gloom of the doorway, with her new haircut, she could understand how they might be confused for each other. Papa was not so easily fooled, of course.

"Come, show me what Elly has done to my little girl," he beckoned her. She approached him, not brashly like the girl who walked out of the salon, but meekly, like the old Rika. "Hmm." He furrowed his brow and cocked his head. "You could be a fashion model. What do you think, Oma?"

"It looks like a bird's nest," Oma muttered. "Martina used to do this awful thing to her hair when she was a teenager. What was it they called it, scraping or teasing or something? A huge pile of fluff, all air and that stinky spray and hair so knotted you could not comb it out without her screaming. These fashions come and go and come. Now, it is back again. How much did you pay for that messy hairdo?"

"Oh, Oma," Rika protested.

"I thought so," Oma nodded her head. "Way too much. Next time, you ask me. I can put some curl into your hair, like I do for Martina. Now that would be nice. There is nothing wrong with a permanent, mind you. I used to perm my hair, but too old to bother with it now."

"So." Willem interrupted his mother's rant. "Martina tells me you and Elly did some Christmas shopping today. Tell me where you went, what did you buy?" For a moment Rika felt resentful at being interrogated, but she knew he just wanted to know about her day. She sat on the floor next to his chair and proceeded to tell him. Meanwhile, Oma sat in her chair, humming softly while she knitted. She was still knitting when Rika said goodnight to change into her barn clothes. She was in such a good mood, she found herself singing as she tossed hay to the sheep, and she wished them a good night before she shut the barn doors. She was still humming and smiling when she slipped into bed.

Chapter Nineteen

The eve of St. Nicolas's birthday fell in the middle of the week. An expanded van Wijk family and Syd celebrated, with the special dinner including a new batch of *pepernoten* made by Oma. Rika noticed that Oma had only tasted one of the cookies she had made the past weekend, so she assumed they did not meet with her grandmother's approval. That was fine with her; she was beginning to share Elly's disdain for the kitchen. If she was such a bad cook, perhaps no one would ask her to make any food for them.

The two girls giggled and whispered their way through dinner, laughing quietly at their own jokes and rolling their eyes at the conversations around them. They had slipped back into their childish skins, carefree and light, silly and cheeky. Oma frowned at them from time to time, but that only encouraged the girls. When Willem finally raised his eyebrows at Rika, she asked if she and Elly might be excused from the table. The adults seemed relieved to watch them run out of the room, giggling hysterically all the way into Rika's bedroom. The girls stayed up late into the night, listening to music, reminiscing about earlier visits, comparing their dreams and all the things cousins talk about.

The next evening, when Martina and Willem announced that they were going to town for some Christmas shopping, Elly asked if she could join them. After a whispered conversation between the adults, they agreed to take her along.

Rika had been at school that day and was happy to remain at home. She was exhausted from her late nights and early mornings. Anyway, she found shopping at that time of year and dealing with crowds more stressful than usual. Hanging out with Elly was fun, but keeping up with her cousin drained Rika's energy. And she hated the pitying glances Elly sent her way whenever she put on her chore clothes to take care of the sheep. She would have to talk to Papa soon about selling the flock, and she didn't expect he'd protest too much. From time to time, since the dogs had gone, she'd forgotten to feed or water the sheep, and Papa had had to remind her. She noticed that he was becoming more impatient with her, although he was in a better mood since their visitors had arrived.

Rika had an evening alone with Oma ahead of her. After chores, she joined Oma in the living room, where her grandmother was crocheting under the light of the floor lamp. Rika sighed and picked up a fashion magazine that Elly had given her to read. It was in Dutch, but Rika could understand most of what was written. When she could not interpret a critical word, she asked her grandmother.

"You have forgotten so much Dutch."

"Only the harder words, Oma, the ones I don't use every day. Papa and I usually talk in English anyway, but I can still read it, mostly."

"I wish your papa had never left us," Oma sniffed. "It was my fault, you know. Only one farm, and two sons. Your Oom Dirk was the oldest—it was his right to take over the farm. But your father is the more generous of the two. You know, if we had given the farm to Willem,

Dirk would never have forgiven us. We would have lost him to our family. Sometimes we have to make such hard choices, Rika."

Rika nodded, with only a brief glance up from her magazine. She had heard this story before, and she did not want her grandmother to get all weepy on her. Rika made a big show of yawning, thinking this was probably a good time to excuse herself and go to bed.

"Instead, we have lost your family. That is too bitter for me to think about. And with your mother gone. I wish Willem had come back home and brought you with him when she died. But of course, he had no farm to come back to. He would have had to look for different work. No, I do not blame him for staying."

As Rika was about to open her mouth to say goodnight, Oma said, "So, Rika, did you like my *pepernoten*?"

"Oma, they were delicious."

"I noticed you only had two." She shook her head. "But my *pepernoten* are not nearly as good as Beatrix Dykstra's. She is a widow back in Holland, a good friend of our family. A splendid cook, that Beatrix, and famous in our area for her wedding cakes and pastries. That is what she does for a living, she runs a small bakery in Muiden. Mostly cakes and cookies, some bread. She and Martina went to school together, you know. We think your papa should meet Beatrix, they would get along well together. This Syd girl is much too young for him," she huffed. "And not even Dutch."

For a moment Rika considered protesting, but she couldn't imagine her father marrying anyone just then. "Is Beatrix the same age as Aunt Martina?"

"A year younger, I think."

"She is five years *older* than Papa?"

"Five years is nothing! We women outlive men all the time. I have been a widow ten years, and I am not anywhere near ready for my dirt nap yet, young lady." She paused to catch her breath. "Anyway, I think Beatrix would make a fine wife for Willem. And it would be nice for him to have a son to raise. Who knows, perhaps they could have more children together. Your poor mother could not have any more—Rika, where are you going?"

Rika stormed into her bedroom and slammed the door shut. She could not stand to hear any more, but she did not have the nerve to contradict her grandmother, much as she wanted to. Oma was calling to her, at first with insistence, then with concern in her voice. Good, she thought, let the old busybody worry. I won't have her talking about Papa like that, not in front of me.

And Mama, how could she even talk about Mama? Rika felt her head pounding with pressure and tears sprang out of her eyes. Poor Mama. Why couldn't she be here to stop all of this from happening? She could have made everything work. Why did Mama have to die? Why? Why? How could she leave? Now the tears were gushing and she could not stop them. She put a pillow over her head so Oma wouldn't hear her wretched sobs.

Chapter Twenty

Elly made it plain on numerous occasions that she found life on Willemrika Farm a total bore and had been pestering Rika about going out to a party or a dance. After asking around at school, Errol told Rika about a party on Friday night at the home of his friend Graham in Charlottetown. Errol was delighted that Rika was interested in coming out again and was happy to include her Dutch cousin. Rika felt herself blushing at his enthusiasm. She could hardly believe she had been so bold as to invite herself and someone else to a party.

"That sounds fine to me," Willem agreed when Rika had asked him. "Since Martina and I are going into town tomorrow, we can drop you off and I can pick you up later. Will that work?"

Bitter memories about the last time she had made pickup arrangements flashed across her mind. "Sure, I guess," she shrugged, but imagined Elly would not be keen on such a tight rein.

Elly surprised her by dismissing any concerns with a simple, "We'll manage it." What did she mean by that? Rika wondered. It didn't matter. In Willem's eyes, apparently, Elly could do no wrong. She was his beloved niece.

After sleeping in until nearly noon, Elly spent the next

few hours preparing for the party. By four that afternoon, Rika had been struggling with her hair for hours, and she still couldn't get it quite right. Willem thought it looked the same as when she had returned from the hair salon, but Rika was unconvinced. What did he know about the latest hairstyles?

Elly insisted that Rika start all over. So she washed her hair for the third time that day and loaded it with gel, then Elly carefully shaped and held the coiffure in place while Rika operated the hairdryer. How, she wondered, was she ever going to do this by herself once her cousin was gone? A work of art to be created in the morning and destroyed each night. But once the last strand was in place, they were both pleased with the results of their arm-aching efforts.

Then Elly applied Rika's makeup. Her nerves on edge, Rika giggled as her cousin plastered and painted it on, layer after layer, another masterpiece she could never reproduce on her own. "Juliana showed me how it's done for the runway models, darling," Elly assured her, waving a small brush in the air. "She learned by watching the pros. They are true artists, you know. It's a bit like being a sculptor, actually. There! Take a look at my amazing creation!" She handed Rika a mirror. Rika gasped—she hardly recognized herself. The apparition staring back from the mirror looked like a duplicate of Elly and the models in her magazines.

"Look how grown up Rika is now," her aunt gushed as Rika twirled in front of her for inspection. "You will not be too cold in just that jacket and skirt? Should you not wear an overcoat?" she asked.

"Mama! The tights, see the tights? Very thick, very warm. And we have these gigantic scarves, see?" Elly pointed to each item on Rika and herself, crossing her eyes when she glanced at her cousin.

"Ya, but it is so much colder here than back home. Willem, can you talk them into wearing warmer clothes? It must be ten below outside."

"Martina, you worry enough for six mothers." Willem chuckled and patted his sister's back. "Anyway, they will be in a car, then in a house, then back in a warm car. I think they will be fine. Right, girls?" he said, winking at them.

Elly launched herself at her uncle and wrapped her arms around him. "Thank you, Oom, you understand. You are uber-cool, you know?" Elly and Rika both snickered at Willem's quizzical expression.

Willem, Martina, and Syd were going out to a nice restaurant for supper that evening. Oma Wilma had opted to stay home to see what nonsense Canadians watched for entertainment on television.

"Okay, girls, ready?" Willem asked, and they all paraded outside into the crisp, chilly night. Willem and Martina drove them into town and dropped them off at Graham's. Once inside, Rika was relieved to see that Errol was already there. She introduced him to Elly and studied her cousin's response. Elly acted nonchalant, but Rika could tell she was impressed.

"So, Errol, what do they have to drink here? Or smoke? You do have pot here on PEI, don't you?" she asked, pouting. "Or do you call it weed? You know, marijuana?" She enunciated each syllable, laughing at Errol's wide-eyed expression.

Errol glanced at Rika and gave her an apologetic half-smile. Rika wished she could melt into the floor and disappear altogether. This was not a good start. What was she thinking, bringing Elly to a party hosted by a sixteen-year-old kid she didn't even know, whose parents were out for the evening but could show up any time? Of course there wouldn't be any weed here, or liquor for them to drink, unless they had brought their own.

And judging by the absence of ashtrays, this was a non-smoking household, for which Rika was relieved. She detested cigarette smoke.

"Umm, I'll check with Graham. I think there's some beer out back, but you might have to go outside to drink it. Let me find out," he said, and trotted off. Inside the living room where they stood, there were another dozen or so kids, all around Rika's age. Some were standing, some sitting, but they all suddenly seemed so young. This had been a big mistake and Elly would never let her live it down.

"God, Rika, no one's even smoking. What kind of shitty party is this?" Elly said in Dutch, frowning at her cousin.

"We're underage, Elly. Maybe if the parents were out of town for the weekend, there might be more going on, but this is a young crowd. Maybe too young for you, eh?" Rika said.

"No smoking, no drinking. This is a drag, we can't stay here. Come on, let's go," Elly urged.

"Go where?"

"Anywhere but here. Let's go to a club or something. I saw at least two when we were in town on Monday," Elly said.

"We couldn't get in," Rika protested. "I'm barely fifteen. I'll get carded!"

"What? What is carded?" Elly asked.

"You know, they'll look at my ID. If they serve liquor in a club, you have to be at least nineteen to get in. And you're just seventeen—we'll never get in!"

"My dear, naive, innocent little cousin," Elly said, taking Rika by the shoulders and staring hard at her. "Have you looked in a mirror lately?" She dropped her arms and opened them wide, smirking. "Do I look my age? Do I? I hope I didn't waste all my time working on you this afternoon."

Rika sighed. Elly most certainly could pass for a twenty-something. If she herself looked anything even close, she'd pass, too.

"Right, we're gone," Elly said with a curt nod. "How far to town from here?"

"I don't know. Maybe twenty, thirty minutes to walk," Rika suggested.

"That's too long. We'll call a taxi. Find me a phone-book, Rika," she ordered. Rika found one in the kitchen and brought it to Elly. While she was on her cell phone, Errol returned.

"Does your cousin still want a beer? The guys said they'd keep one for her—if she's still interested," Errol said, and tilted his head toward Elly. "Who's she calling?"

"Uh, she doesn't want to stay, Errol," Rika started to explain. "Sorry, I—"

"Okay, the taxi will be here in five minutes, Rika. Oh, hi there. We can't stay, I'm sorry. Tell your friend he has a nice house." With that she grabbed Rika's arm and dragged her to the front door. Rika looked back at Errol, shrugging her shoulders. He looked confused, and Rika suddenly realized that she really wanted to stay, even though Errol was the only person she knew at the party. Or perhaps because he was the only person she knew.

Errol frowned, but raised his hand. "See you next week?"

Rika raised her own hand, her eyes wide, and attempted a smile. "Yeah, I'm back on Tuesday. Thanks. For inviting us."

"Sure," he said, but he was not smiling when he turned away.

Before Rika could say another word, Elly had pushed her outside and shut the door behind them. She felt powerless to contradict her cousin, and was resigned to stay close to her. And if possible, to keep them both out of trouble.

Rika had never been inside a club. She stared up at the blinking pink lights spelling out "Mussel Cave" as they walked through the smoked-glass doors. Elly's prediction proved true: they were not carded, just stamped and waved in after paying cover. It was dark and so loud inside that Rika's knees almost buckled as she walked in. A live band played on a raised platform at the back, and a bar lined most of the right side. The few tables scattered around were full, and a throng of bodies on the dance floor in front of the band pulsated under flashing strobe lights. The entire place was throbbing, like a huge, pumping heart.

Elly thrust her arms into the air. "This is more like it!" she shouted, although Rika barely heard her. "I'm buying you a drink!"

"You'll have to," Rika answered, "I have no money with me." But Elly was already pushing her way to the bar. Rika stayed as close behind as she could, terrified that they might be separated. What if Elly found someone she wanted to dance with, or go smoke a joint with? No, Elly wouldn't abandon her—would she?

Her cousin was obviously in her element. Elly's smile was electric, her body vibrated, she seemed to grow a head taller. Elly in Wonderland. She ordered two drinks and handed one to Rika. "Cheers!" she said, raising her wine-coloured drink in the air. Rika also raised her glass, afraid to ask what she was about to drink. She took a tentative sip. At first, it tasted like weak cranberry juice, then the searing heat that followed made her gasp. Elly slapped her on the back. "Don't worry, you'll catch on. Sip slowly, you'll be fine."

Rika wasn't so sure. Why would anyone want to have their throats and gullets burned by alcohol over and over again? But she didn't dare put down her drink and walk out the door and back to the quiet party in the suburbs. For one thing, she didn't want to leave Elly alone—she was afraid for her. Elly's eyes had now gone wild, she was swinging her head around like a lizard, appraising the crowd, as if she was a starving predator planning her kill. Rika took another sip and winced.

"Hey!" someone shouted in her ear. Rika turned her head to see a short, muscular man with close-cropped red hair and sunglasses. His face was inches away from hers, and he reeked of cigarettes and alcohol. Rika tried to step back but realized there was nowhere to move. "I haven't seen you here before. You from 'round here?" he slurred.

Rika looked around for Elly, but she was gone. She whipped her head back to the man. "No, I am from Holland, just visiting my cousin. I must find her," she said in her best Dutch accent, and with the drink gripped in her hand, she squeezed herself into the crowd. Where was Elly? How would she ever find her in this huge, black cavern? Rika gulped down the rest of her drink and pushed herself through to the dance floor. She was tall enough that she could see above most of the people around her. There was Elly, gyrating and jumping, practically on the stage with the band. Rika couldn't tell if she had a partner or was dancing by herself. She took a deep breath and plunged into the wave of bodies. By the time she reached Elly, she felt like her brain had been liquefied by the pounding speakers. Elly screamed at her, jumped up and down several times then grabbed Rika's hands. Rika shook her head. No, she did not want to dance, and certainly not this close to the band! Elly laughed and reached into a pocket then shoved some money into Rika's hand.

"Buy us some drinks!" she shouted into her ear. "Anything you like! Cosmos are good. You know, what you were drinking before!" At least that was what she thought Elly said. Rika shook her head, but made her way back out through the dancers and toward the end of the bar, as far from the band as she could go. She really didn't want another drink, but she didn't want to annoy her cousin, or leave her alone, either.

"Two cosmos, please!" she shouted at the bartender.

"Two cosmos coming up!" he shouted back.

By the time Rika had finished her second drink and delivered one to Elly, she was ready to use the washroom. She found it back behind the bar, several stalls, all painted black. The checkerboard pattern of black-and-white floor tiles made her dizzy when she looked down. Rika sniffed. The air in the washroom was hazy with smoke. Smoking in all public buildings was against the law, so how could this be? She sniffed again—it was *not* cigarette smoke.

Elly would be happy, though. In fact, she could probably find someone to sell her some pot tonight, or maybe just give it to her. Elly had boasted how recreational drugs were legal in Holland, and complained how backward Canada was. She told Rika that she and her friends had no trouble finding what they wanted anytime they wished. All of a sudden, Rika felt responsible for Elly, felt she had to find her immediately and get her out of here. But how was she going to do it? Elly would never listen to her. Elly wouldn't listen to anyone. It was obvious she didn't respect her mother. Oh dear, poor Aunt Martina. Rika didn't want to let her down.

She hurried back out into the throngs and began her search for Elly. But she was nowhere to be found. Rika ran outside and noticed several small clusters of people up and down the street on the sidewalk. She shivered in the cold, wishing she was in her overalls and insulated boots instead of these tights and trendy thin leather jacket. At that moment, she was feeling far from fashionable and closer to a meltdown. Then she heard Elly's unmistakable laugh. There she was, leaning against a truck, smoking with a group of guys. They looked like bikers, fitted out in studded black leather from top to toe, but Rika didn't care who they were.

"Elly!" Rika stepped in front of her.

"Whoa, it's another one! You from the old country, too, blondie?" A leather-clad smoker peered at her through his sunglasses.

Elly blew out a stream of smoke and laughed again. "Hey, guys, this is my little cousin, Hendrika. She's cute, isn't she? Not bad for a little farm girl, huh?"

"Farmer's daughter, eh?" A tall, hefty man looked Rika up and down. "Wanna go for a ride, little girl?" he asked and chuckled.

Rika shivered and stepped closer to her cousin. "Elly, we have to go home. Now," she said as firmly as she could. Suddenly Elly's face split into two. Rika shook her head and reached out for the hood of the truck to steady herself.

"I think your cousin is under the influence, Louella," one of them snickered.

"Elly," Rika whispered, realizing that she had to try something different. "I don't feel well. Can we go home? Please?"

"Aw dammit, Rika. I'm finally, after a whole boring, deadly week, starting to have some fun here, and you pull this on me. Honest to God, I'm never taking you out again. You are such a drag." Rika did not raise her head to look at Elly.

"We can give you a lift home, ladies," one of the men offered.

Rika stiffened and prepared to respond, but Elly beat her to it. "Thanks, guys, but we'd better call our regular ride or her daddy will get upset. You know how it is. She's really too young to be out, and I don't want to get her in trouble. The things I have to do sometimes, the sacrifices," she sighed.

"Suit yourself," the big fellow said. They all dropped their smokes, ground them into the pavement and walked back into the club.

Rika lifted her head. The spinning had stopped for the moment but the blinking lights over the club door made her head ache. "Should we go back to Graham's first?" she asked.

"Don't be stupid, Rika. It's past midnight and all those little kids will be tucked into their beds. Here, give me the number. Don't worry, I'll tell your papa this was all my idea."

Elly and Rika stood shivering, not speaking, on a nearby corner until they saw Willem's truck pull up and stop. Elly practically shoved Rika into the seat ahead of her. Willem told them to buckle up, but said nothing more. Rika kept her eyes straight ahead as she sat in the middle, but her head pounded and she began to feel nauseated. Once they were out on the main highway she blurted out, "I think I'm going to be sick." Willem pulled over to the side immediately and Elly had her door open before the truck stopped moving. Rika managed to get out before she started to retch into the ditch, while Willem held her with an arm around her waist and another hand grasping the back of her jacket. When she was done, she tried to straighten up but could feel her knees wobbling beneath her.

"I still don't feel well, Papa," she complained.

"No, I do not imagine you do," he said. "We will be home soon. Now, do you think there is anything left in your stomach?"

"I don't think so."

"Good, home we go. Martina is worried sick." Elly was already sitting in the middle of the seat, shivering and hugging herself, when Willem helped Rika back inside.

Elly never said another word that night, not even to thank her uncle for the ride home. Once inside the house, Willem walked Rika into the living room and sat her down on one of the overstuffed chairs. He then sat himself opposite her and folded his hands on his lap.

"Now, young lady, I need some straight answers from you," he began, looking directly at her.

Rika raised her head and stared back at him.

"Were you drinking alcohol?"

She paused. "Yes."

"Why?"

"Elly didn't like the party and wanted to go to a club. She bought me a drink, so I had to drink it."

"No, you did not have to drink it. You could have said, 'No thank you'. I am sure Elly would not mind."

"Oh, Papa, you don't know Elly. She wanted to have some fun, I didn't want to ruin it for her. I only had two, Papa, and I didn't even like it."

"Rika, Rika," Willem sighed. "Why do you do this to yourself? To me?"

"I don't mean to hurt you, Papa. I just wanted to have some fun. I've been so miserable." Rika dropped her head, blinking hard, and grasped her hands together.

"Rika, my child, I want you to be happy, too. I know you have suffered through some terrible mishaps these past few months. And perhaps you have been troubled by other bad memories from long ago. But I, too, have a right to some happiness. Will you finally let your mother go?"

Rika glared at him. "What does Mama have to do with anything?"

"I think she has a lot to do with how you are feeling right now, and how you have been acting for a long time. And you are thinking a lot about yourself these days. All I ask is that you consider some of the other people in your life. You are not alone on this earth. You depend on others, and others depend on you. What you do and how you feel affects my happiness as well as yours. When you have finished moping and feeling sorry for yourself, think about it. That is all I ask." He got up to leave the room. "And thank you for being honest with me. Now do yourself a big favour, and be honest with yourself. Goodnight, Rika."

Chapter Twenty One

Rika had trouble falling asleep that night, and once she did, she was restless. Towards dawn her troubling dreams reappeared. This time she was in a cold room with tall, smooth, steel walls and no doors. The room was empty except for a metal table in the very centre. Below the table was a cage. She heard an animal growling inside the cage, but gradually the noise grew louder and finally turned into a frantic bark. First the cage began to tremble, then the entire table shook as the barking changed into a roar. Rika backed up to a wall and looked desperately for a door. Then she noticed blood oozing out from the cage.

She awoke with a start and opened her eyes to morning light. But the roaring continued, and when she looked at the window, she realized it was white with snow. Periodic gusts of wind shook the house and rattled the roof shingles. Rika sank under her bed covers as a blizzard raged outside. Ugh, she thought, it was Saturday. Why couldn't the bad weather hit during the school week so they could have a snow day?

She recalled the night out with Elly and shuddered. Her throat was dry and her eyes smarted, probably from the smoky washroom, or maybe from the liquor. Rika had only ever tasted wine on two occasions before, and she had decided that it was highly overrated. She glanced at the clock on her dresser. It flashed 4:33. She wondered how long their power had been off, and what time it really was, but it didn't matter. She slipped under the covers again. When she awoke again and sat up, she felt a strong pulse or two behind her eyes and worried that the headache would return. Could she get a hangover from just two drinks? But nothing more happened.

As she passed by the dresser mirror, she winced. With makeup smeared around her eyes and swollen cheeks, she resembled a pale raccoon. Was she having an allergic reaction? It took her some time to scrub off all traces of the eye makeup Elly had applied the day before. She remembered trying to wash her face before bed, but the mascara was tenacious. She stared at her chipped blue nails. That would have to go, too. What had she been thinking?

Rika came down to an empty kitchen. She could hear Oma and Aunt Martina talking quietly in the living room. She poured herself a glass of orange juice and decided to face them. It would have to happen sooner or later, she thought as she walked in.

"Ah, Rika my dear, how are you this morning? Your papa told us you were not feeling well last night," her aunt said, concern lining her face. Oma looked up and grunted but continued to crochet.

Rika sat on a stool facing her aunt. "I'm okay now, Auntie. A little tired, maybe. I didn't sleep well."

"I know, darling. That wind is fearsome. Willem says the storm should pass by early afternoon. At least the electricity is back on. But, anyway, you have a wood stove, so you will not freeze here," she said, shivering and pulling her wool wrap tighter around her shoulders.

"Perhaps," Oma joined in. "But you are so far from anyone, what if there was an emergency and you could not get to a doctor or hospital? I do not like this one bit. You should live closer to town," she grumbled.

"We have a tractor, Oma. Papa and I can both drive it, and it has a snow blower and a plough, so we can get out if we really need to."

"But just two of you. I worry, really. You have this big house—perhaps you can take boarders. You know, some farm help, a strong young man, or even a small family."

Martina looked at her mother and smiled. She was about to say something, glanced over at Rika, then seemed to change her mind.

Rika felt uncomfortable. Aunt Martina had said nothing about Elly so far. "Is Elly up yet?" she asked.

"No, dear, she had a terrible headache this morning. I gave her some Tylenol and she went back to sleep." She paused. "Rika, have you had any breakfast? Come, come, I'll make you something." She stood up and put her hand out for her niece, who was hunched over on the short stool. Rika wanted to protest, but the look in her aunt's eyes implored the girl to follow along, so she did. In the kitchen, Martina asked Rika what she would like and went to work making toast, which was the only thing Rika felt her stomach would tolerate.

Martina poured herself a cup of coffee, then sat down at the table. Rika picked up a triangle of toast and nibbled from the buttered centre, watching her aunt from the corner of her eyes.

"My dear child," she began in a quiet voice, patting Rika's arm. "I know what happened last night. Elly did not say a thing to me, I just know," she said, her voice wavering. "Elly has some new friends back at home, friends we wish she did not spend time with. But she will not listen to us. If we try to control her or make the rules too strict, we are afraid to drive her away from us and straight into the arms of corruption. Anton and I pray this is only a stage. Juliana was like this when she was Elly's age, and she is fine now, living on her own, a good job, a steady boyfriend. Juliana will be home next week, just before Christmas. She promised she would talk to her sister before Elly does something foolish or dangerous." She paused again, and sipped her coffee, her hands trembling.

"Rika, I know it was her idea to go to the club, to buy you drinks, and I should never have let her go out with you alone. If anything had happened to you, oh! I would never forgive myself!" At that she covered her face and began to cry. Rika could feel tears edging up in her own eyes. She hated to see her aunt this pained by her cousin's actions. And hers, too, she thought.

"So no matter what Elly says to you, I know you did nothing wrong. You are a good girl, Rika. Willem has done well by you. But more than that, you are a gem, and it is easy to see why he is so proud of you and loves you so much. We all do." She sniffled and patted Rika's arm again.

Rika swallowed and put down her toast. "Thank you, Auntie. That means a lot to me," she said, blinking away the tears. She stood up and gave her aunt a kiss on her warm, wet cheek.

Rika spent the rest of the morning in the sheep barn. She had always enjoyed being inside with the sheep during blizzards. The barn boards shook and groaned when the wind struck them, but Rika knew they would hold. She was safe inside, snuggled against the hay, out of the wind, and in between gusts she was soothed by the sounds of sheep chewing and rustling in the straw. Several sheep came to see her, to sniff her face, her coat, her boots. The younger ones occasionally nibbled on her wrecked hair. She wondered what it tasted like with all that gel in it. Yuck. She scratched under their chins and behind their ears while they leaned into her. Just like Vasi used to do.

Rika supposed he was probably back in the kennel at Mrs. Brewer's. She wondered what Vasi was thinking. Did he miss his leg? Did it hurt? Syd said he could run and jump and do all the things he had done before. A human would never be able to heal that fast, she thought. But would he ever be a stud dog with only three legs? She fretted about how much it had cost to pull him through. Rika was determined to pay for it, no matter how long it took her. Syd had mentioned once that if she was interested, she could work part-time at the clinic. Between that and selling her sheep, she could make enough money to pay everyone back.

But what about Vasi? What would happen to him now? She wondered if he missed the sheep. Did he miss her? Ha! He probably hated her for what she'd done to him, she thought bitterly.

But, on reflection, Rika knew that Vasi would not associate what happened to him with her. He'd been doing his job, chasing away a predator, having a great time. The dogs loved their work more than anything, Mrs. Brewer had said. Syd had said the same thing, come to think of it. When that defensive drive kicked in, the rest of the world disappeared around them. That's why he didn't notice the truck belting down the road straight at him.

Rika wiped her eyes. "You guys probably miss him, too. I can't let you out at night anymore without him. You've lost your freedom. Or do you even remember that far back with those sheepy little brains of yours?"

A bright ray of light shot through a window onto the hay beside Rika. The storm had broken, the sun was winning the battle of the skies. Even the wind had died down somewhat, she thought. She got up and brushed the bits of hay from her overalls. Their Dutch visitors were leaving on Monday and Rika had not finished her Christmas gift shopping for them yet. She wondered what Liz was up to this afternoon. It seemed like years since she had spent any time with her best friend. She had some catching up and making up to do. It was time to make a call.

Chapter Twenty-Two

By Sunday morning, the weather had changed completely from twenty-four hours earlier. The sun had won the latest skirmish and had commanded the air to be still and warm, like spring in December. The entire van Wijk family crowded into the rental car for the trip to church. They were quieter than usual, perhaps reflecting on their last full day together. Elly had not said a word to Rika since Friday night. In fact, she had shut herself in her room for most of Saturday and had spoken to no one. Rika wondered if Aunt Martina had given her a stern lecture, something about being responsible for her innocent younger cousin. She imagined that Elly would blame her entirely for how things had turned out. Elly was the ice queen herself this morning, her white-blond icicles of hair framing a pale face pierced with frosty blue eyes. Rika felt uneasy in her presence and was glad that her aunt sat between the two of them.

After the service, Willem stopped just inside the foyer of the church to introduce a few friends to his sister and mother. Elly kept on walking out the doors and motioned for Rika to follow her. Rika joined her, nervous about what Elly might say. Something sarcastic, no doubt. She steeled herself.

"Listen, Rika, I thought I'd better tell you this before we leave tomorrow. It's about your papa," she said, her lips curving up in a nasty smile.

"Mm-hmm?" was all Rika could manage with her teeth clenched.

"That night I went shopping with him and Mama, they spent a lot of time in a snazzy jewellery store. They told me to go browsing, but I hung around where they couldn't see me. I could tell they were being sneaky. Do you know what they were looking at?" she asked with a smirk.

"No, but you're going to tell me, aren't you?" Rika said.

"Of course. It's something you should know. I mean, I wouldn't want this kind of surprise myself, so it's the least I can do for you—cousin," she almost snarled.

Rika willed her frozen legs to start moving, to walk away and show Elly that she did not care. But she found her feet stuck to the pavement.

"Diamond rings! That's what they were looking at. After they left, I walked over to the counter to make sure. And I'm pretty sure your papa bought one. So, you know what *that* means. And you told me he wouldn't get engaged without consulting you first," she taunted.

Rika was speechless for a moment. "I never said that!" she hissed. She tried to remember what she had said to her cousin nearly a week ago. "I said he wouldn't get married without letting me know. And he's not married yet. And, anyway, he can get married without my permission. What's the big deal?"

"The big deal is that you *do* care, and that your dear papa hasn't shared any of his plans with you, but he has with my mother. You think you're so tight, you and your papa. You're so naive, little cousin. And not very bright, either!" With that she wheeled around and headed for the car, where Willem was already helping his mother into the front seat.

Rika could practically feel the steam puffing out of her ears. She pressed her lips together and marched after Elly towards the car. Aunt Martina was looking from one girl to the other, but said nothing as she took up her buffer position in the middle of the back seat.

Back at home, Rika changed into her chore clothes and ran off to the barn. She wanted to scream in frustration, but she would never give Elly the satisfaction of hearing her. She did not trust Elly, and half expected to see her lurking around the barn. It was December 10, Rika's fifteenth birthday. Except for Liz, who had wished her a happy birthday yesterday, no one, not even Papa, had acknowledged her special day.

Elly was probably right, damn her. Papa was so wrapped up in their visitors, in Syd, that Rika had fallen by the wayside. But how could he have forgotten her birthday? She was his only child. It was unforgivable!

"Aargh!" she choked out and kicked a bale of hay. There was no way she planned to spend the day with her loving family, the family who had forgotten her fifteenth birthday. Maybe she should take the gifts she had bought them and bring them over to Liz's. She could give them away to a charity. Anyone would be more deserving than her family.

When she calmed down enough to return to the house, she noticed that her aunt and Oma had already put lunch on the table. She thought sadly that she had no quarrel with them, and it would be rude to leave the house on their last day together. Instead, after lunch, she excused herself to do the homework she had missed during the past week. She figured no one would complain about that.

Rika heard supper preparations beginning sooner than usual that afternoon. Aunt Martina had announced earlier that they were having a large ham and scalloped potatoes, one of Rika's favourite meals. By the time supper was ready, Rika emerged from her self-imposed exile. When she passed by a mirror she was aware that her hair had returned to its limp default state. The glamorous Rika was gone, and she was surprised at her sense of relief.

She decided to put on a brave, cheerful face for the benefit of her aunt and grandmother. Still, not a word about her birthday. A cherry pie was cooling on the counter in the kitchen, not a cake. Elly kept stealing glances at her, as if she was waiting for Rika to crack. Rika simply smiled at her while Papa beamed at them from the head of the table. He probably thought she was happy. Ha!

While Aunt Martina was in the kitchen slicing the pie and Rika cleared dishes from the table, she noticed headlights flash through the kitchen window. Syd soon appeared at the door. "I'm late, aren't I?" she asked in a cheerful voice. "Had an emergency to deal with, sorry!"

"It is no problem," Martina assured her. "I will make a plate for you. Rika, would you please take this pie into the dining room, and please sit. We will be there in a moment."

Rika brought the pie in and placed it near Martina's place at the table. She heard the back door to the kitchen open and close a couple of times and wondered what was keeping Martina and Syd. She did not know Syd had been invited to their farewell family dinner. But then, she'd be part of the family soon enough. Keeping secrets from Rika seemed to be the new pattern.

Suddenly the lights went out in the dining room. "Uh-oh," Willem said, and laughed. A glow from the kitchen grew brighter until a row of flickering candles appeared suspended in the doorway. Willem began singing and the rest joined him.

"Happy birthday to Rika, happy birthday to you!" Everyone clapped and cheered and her aunt hugged and kissed her. The lights went back on. By then Rika had recovered enough to be wearing a huge smile. She didn't know whether she should feel annoyed with them, grateful, or just plain stupid to have missed all the clues. Maybe Papa was right: she had been way too self-absorbed lately.

Rika cut the first piece of the German chocolate cake, placed it on a dish, and offered it to her grandmother. But Oma waved it aside, saying she could not eat a sweet so soon after such a big dinner. Rika looked around for Elly, but she had vanished, probably when the lights were out. Hmph, thought Rika; she didn't have the stomach for a piece of happiness. After all the others had cake and refused second helpings, the gifts came out. The first one was from Oma. An oat bag, eight inches wide and two feet long, covered in a festive cotton print. Oma explained that Rika could warm it in the microwave before she went to bed and wrap it around her cold feet on those chilly winter nights. Or, she could use it as a cold compress if she had injured muscles or a headache. And all this time Rika had thought oats were just for eating!

Willem's gift was a small one. In fact, he took it out of his shirt pocket and placed the tiny red velvet box in Rika's hand. She was astonished. He never gave her jewellery, mainly because she had never asked for any and didn't show much interest in bling. But he was also a practical man and considered most jewellery frivolous. She opened the box and was dazzled by an ornately carved silver and turquoise ring.

"Papa, this is so beautiful." She did not know what else to say.

"I hope you like it, Rika. Turquoise is one of the December birthstones. We did some research on it and discovered that the name for this mineral may have come from the French word for the country of Turkey, *Turquie*. Long ago, it was believed that this is where turquoise was to be found. It is just a little story, but interesting."

"Yes, so interesting, and gorgeous. Thank you, Papa!" Rika rose from her chair and gave her father a tight hug.

"There is one more gift, Rika," Papa said. At that, Syd leaned over and handed Rika an envelope. Rika opened it and read the card. Her eyes widened and her mouth dropped open.

"A Border Collie puppy? Oh my God! When?" Rika's words spilled out without thinking. She had been taught never to use the word *God* in an exclamation, but only Oma raised her eyebrows. The rest were too busy laughing and enjoying her surprise.

"Not until spring. Which is a perfect time for a new pup, don't you think?" Syd said.

Rika just nodded her head and laughed with delight. A Border Collie pup, out of Scottish working lines. She had wanted one for so long, and now her wish would come true. She felt an ache between her ribs, above her stomach. What was that? Too much cake? Too much excitement? Or was she worried she'd screw this up, too? No, she had to stop thinking that way. Especially after feeling so dejected all day, and having all those uncharitable thoughts about her father, about Syd, about everyone.

"I—I don't know what to say. Thank you, Syd. I'm—I'm thrilled. This is crazy. This is the most amazing birthday ever! Thank you." She sniffled and wiped the tears from her eyes, grinning the whole time.

As Rika drifted into sleep that night, her head still spinning from all the attention and love, she felt annoyed with herself for not feeling more grateful and content. She needed to stop overanalyzing everything that happened and just accept it. Wasn't that the Buddhist belief? Once, during a discussion of world religions, Liz had talked about becoming a Buddhist. Though she wasn't serious,

Rika wondered if maybe she should consider it herself. The idea made her smile.

Not long after she fell asleep, the old nightmare visited her again. Once more she stood in that cold, metallic room with smooth walls, facing a tall door and standing in oozing red liquid. The liquid was rising higher and higher, and Rika began to panic. She tried to find a way out of this metal chamber, but there was only one door. She was sure the red stuff was oozing out from behind the door. Was it blood? Whose blood? Would she drown if she opened that door? The level was up to her neck now, and she needed to make a decision. It was time, she had to know.

She reached toward the door and grasped the handle. She pulled. Nothing happened. She pulled with all her strength, gasping with exertion, and slowly, inch by inch, the door began to open. She tried to close her eyes, afraid of what she might see, but her eyes would not shut.

Suddenly, the door opened to brilliant white light. The intensity was blinding, but her eyes were still glued open. A tall form stood in front of the blazing light. As her eyes adjusted, she could make out the shape of a woman wrapped in shimmering gold cloth. She could not make out her face, except for the smile. A wide, warm smile. Rika strained to see who it was. The nose began to form, a small, turned-up nose like her own. Then the shining blue eyes came into focus.

"Mama!" she yelled, and woke herself up. Rika's heart raced as she sat up and rubbed her eyes. There was no one in her dark room. Then her door opened and bright light spilled into her eyes. "Ahh!" she shouted, still not fully awake. She felt an arm around her shoulders.

"Rika, it is Papa. Did you have a bad dream?"

"Papa? It's you, it's not—Papa, I dreamt about Mama. It's that nightmare. But this time I opened the door and the blood was gone, and there she was, Papa, she came back. She was smiling. She's okay, Papa." Her father hugged her fiercely, and she clung to him.

"Ya, she is okay, wherever she is. I still miss her, too, Rika. You never stop caring for the ones you have loved. Never." Father and daughter held each other for a few moments longer.

"Will you be all right?" he asked.

"I'll be fine, Papa," Rika sniffled. "I opened the door. It's okay, I'm not afraid."

"Good, nothing to be afraid of. Now sleep well, *m'n kleine meid*." He kissed her forehead and left the room. Rika smiled at the Dutch endearment, words she had not heard in a long time. Farm partners or not, she was still his little girl. She closed her eyes and slept dreamlessly for the remainder of the night.

Chapter Twenty-Three

Rika had arranged to stay home from school on Monday to see her relatives off at the airport. They had protested that morning when she had given them Christmas gifts to take back to Holland. Rika gave Elly's gift to her aunt. Elly would probably throw out the fancy blow-drying brush when she unwrapped it, but Rika didn't want to see it in her garbage bin at home. And maybe, without Rika around, she might even keep it.

In the departure lounge, Rika hugged her aunt for a long time. "Good luck," she whispered, crying openly, disregarding Elly's look of disdain.

Oma was the last to say good-bye. She held Rika's hands and looked up into her eyes, saying, "My little tall one, I hope you will forgive me for anything I may have said to upset you. You are a good daughter to Willem, and I can see that you have been taking good care of each other. I am just an interfering old hen, it comes with the age. You have to forgive an old woman preparing to meet her husband in Heaven. Be good, my child, and kind." Rika leaned down to kiss her cheek, and the floral scent that had greeted her when they first arrived rose up again. With a shock, she realized it was a smell she associated with her own mother. Perhaps a perfume, a special lotion or soap? A scent from Holland only her mother ever wore—and her Oma. Rika smiled through her tears.

"Oma," she whispered. "I will miss you very much. But I'll see you in Holland before you make any other trips, I promise." Her grandmother nodded her head and smiled, then patted Rika's cheek and turned away. Hmm, thought Rika, she doesn't want me to see her cry. Tough old hen.

Elly gave Willem a hug good-bye and merely waved at Rika, who also raised her hand in farewell. "So, send me an email sometime, Rika, now you're connected to the world wide web of horror and intrigue. Oom, you'll be sorry you let her have it. You're spoiling her." And with those words she turned and joined her mother and grandmother as they left for the boarding area. Willem and Rika waited and watched until the plane lifted off.

Rika was back in the barn within minutes of arriving home. Perhaps this was where she'd gone wrong after the accident. She had forsaken the peace and solitude of the barn, of letting the animals feed her soul, calming her when she was sad or hurt or agitated. She mused again about the Buddhist lifestyle. They were vegetarians, so if she decided to be one she'd have to give up eating meat. And would she no longer be able to raise lambs for meat? She calculated she'd end up with a lot of lambs if she kept breeding sheep. Rika wasn't sure she was ready for such a radical change. She laughed out loud, imagining the look on Oma's face if she ever announced such a conversion of faith. Rika, the rebel, ha!

As she sat on the bales of hay, looking down on her flock chewing their cuds, she felt happier than she had in a long while. She could no longer imagine life without her flock. She knew she would figure out a way to repay her debt to Mrs. Brewer. Still, she had a nagging feeling that something was not quite right. Even the thought of having a Border Collie pup didn't fill the gap. What was it? What was missing? She'd reconnected with Liz when they went gift shopping, apologizing for how awful she'd been to her loyal friend. As usual, Liz just shrugged and said she knew it had been a rough time, and had believed that the old Rika would eventually resurface. Liz also assured her that Errol was not easily put off. The two of them had been talking, both worried about Rika, and delighted to see her coming back to herself.

Was it the ring? Elly had said that Papa and Aunt Martina were at the diamond ring counter, that they bought a ring there. Had Elly lied? Rika believed that her cousin was quite capable of it, just to annoy her. But maybe she wasn't lying and maybe Papa had bought her birthday ring on another occasion. He talked about them doing some research on birthstones with someone, saying "we." Probably him and Syd. She would be the one to come up with a story like that, linking Rika's birthstone to Turkey, to the Akbash Dogs from that country. Something didn't add up.

The solution to this math problem was clarified later that evening. After supper, which consisted of birthday food leftovers, Willem invited Rika into the living room. They sat beside each other on the couch.

"Rika, I have something I want to show you."

Rika looked at him with anticipation. Somehow, she felt she could not possibly be surprised by anything he would say or do. Still, he was acting mysterious and his expression was serious. He pulled out a small, dark green velvet box with a rounded top. The colour was exactly the same as the dress Syd had worn at Thanksgiving. Willem opened the lid and many tiny beams of light sprung out of captivity. The diamond ring!

Willem had a hopeful, pleading look on his youthful face. "The old custom is for the man who wishes to marry to ask for permission from the father of the bride. But times are different now, and we are not the usual family.

So I am asking, what do you think of my marrying again?"

Rika took a deep, trembling breath. "To Syd?"

Willem swallowed and nodded his head.

"Oh, Papa!" Rika squealed and kissed her father on the cheek. "Of course!" She could not believe her sense of elation. She only knew she wanted her father to be happy. She felt tears forming and shook her head. "This is so exciting!"

"Well, she might turn me down."

"Do you really think so, Papa? Would it be because of me?" Rika suddenly felt guilty about how rude and thoughtless she'd been toward Syd, worried that she might have ruined her father's chance for happiness.

"No, do not even think that. She loves you, Rika, although you may not have noticed. And I *think* she loves me. We will see if she thinks enough of me to accept my proposal."

"Of course she will, Papa. It's obvious she adores you. I mean, how could she not? Will it be a big wedding? When? Are we inviting all our relatives?"

"Hold on now, young lady. Perhaps we should continue this conversation *after* Syd agrees to marry me. I must admit I am just a little bit superstitious about such things."

"No, you're just old-fashioned, Papa."

When Rika returned to school on Tuesday, it felt like she had been gone for months, like she was starting all over at the beginning of a school year. A certain haze had lifted from her eyes, she could hear everything more clearly, all the colours around her seemed more vibrant. She ate lunch with Errol, who filled her in on the party at Graham's. Apparently, his parents had returned earlier than expected and the beer drinkers were quickly evicted. After that, everyone went home early. She hadn't missed much, he assured her. Rika admitted that her evening was far from wonderful as well, and she was glad she had such loyal and level-headed friends like Errol and Liz. By the end of lunch, they had agreed to see a movie on the weekend, and went off to their respective classes. Rika did not remember taking her seat in French class and could barely concentrate for the rest of the afternoon.

When she arrived home, she noticed that Syd's truck was parked in their driveway. Inside the house, all was quiet. Rika pulled on her overalls, boots, and tam and headed for the dairy barn. She found Syd in a stall with a newborn calf and Papa scrubbing his hands in a bucket of soapy water.

"Did Maybelle have a problem?" Rika asked.

"She just needed a little help," Syd replied and looked up at Rika, beaming as if she was the proud mama cow herself.

"I was in the middle of milking," Willem explained. "So I called in the expert." He grinned at Syd then turned to Rika. "Off to the sheep, are you?" he asked.

"Uh-huh. Unless you need my help here," Rika asked with a grin of her own.

"No, daughter, I think we can manage now. Off with you," he said, and winked at her.

Rika trotted off to the sheep barn. Those two were acting plain silly, she thought. She supposed they were in love, which was good if they were going to get married. She wondered when Papa would pop the question. He had said he didn't know when, it depended on the situation. He wanted it to be just right. She hadn't realized what a romantic nature he had. But then, he was her papa. And since her own romantic stirrings had come to the surface, she felt more sympathetic to that side of him.

Rika walked into the sheep barn and switched on the lights. A few of the sheep baaed at her. One at a time, they stood up, shook themselves, and bleated more loudly.

Rika reached up for a bale of hay to put in the manger. When she looked up, she gasped at the face that stared down at her, just inches from her own. He whimpered, then leapt off the bales, landing on all three legs.

"Vasi! Oh my God, it's you, Vasi! My wonderful, brave dog. Oh, Vasi." She threw her arms around the delighted dog and cried into his mane. "I'm sorry for what I did to you, Vasi. Will you ever forgive me?" But she knew forgiveness wasn't part of his language, nor was blame. He loved her just the same, no matter what she said or did or what her hair or clothes looked like. She sat down in the straw and Vasi lay down next to her. Rika massaged his body, from face to tail, being very gentle near the scars of his amputated leg. Vasi closed his eyes and lazily thumped his tail.

Rika didn't know how long she had been out in the barn when she heard the door open. "May we interrupt you?" Willem asked.

Rika looked up. "Sure, we're just hanging out. Why didn't you tell me about Vasi, Syd?"

"Oh, I thought we'd surprise you. I hope you don't mind." She crouched on the other side of Vasi and stroked his back. A deep sigh escaped from the prone dog.

"No, it was a great surprise, just a bit of a shock. What about Mrs. Brewer? Will she let me have him back? Does she even trust me with Vasi?" Rika looked downcast, and stopped petting for a moment. Vasi reached up with a paw and hooked her hand.

"Since he's mended so well, she'd rather he stayed here, if it's okay with you. We think he should be able to breed naturally. But if it's a problem, there's always artificial insemination. No, he belongs here, everybody agrees on that. What happened was an accident, Rika, it's in the past, and we don't need to dwell on it. Okay?" Rika nodded her head, not quite believing all she just heard, struggling to keep the tears at bay.

"And while we're on the topic of surprises, look at what your father gave me!" Syd waved her left hand in front of Rika. The beams of light danced on her finger, reflected in her twinkling eyes. "He just couldn't wait. Proposed right in the dairy barn."

"And to my great delight, she accepted!" Willem knelt beside Syd and took her hand in his. For an awkward moment, no one said anything.

Finally, Rika broke the silence. "Excellent. Let's plan a party!"

Syd and Willem exchanged huge grins of joy, then Syd clapped her hands. She stared at Rika with an intensity the girl had not seen before. "So you're okay with this, Rika?"

Rika nodded her head, then looked back down at Vasi who thumped his tail and panted. "Yup, I'm all for it. You two deserve each other. I mean that only in the nicest way, of course," she smiled up at them.

Syd expelled the breath she had been holding in. "I have one more request for you, Rika."

"Okay." Was she going to be asked to be a bridesmaid, or maybe to make the wedding cake?

"Did you come up with any ideas for a new clinic name?" she asked.

"Uh, no, sorry Syd, I haven't been thinking a whole lot about it lately, I, uh..." Rika petered out, thinking how selfish and self-centred she had been the last few weeks. She dropped her head in shame.

"Oh, that's fine, I understand completely," Syd assured her. "I had a thought, though, just the other day. I was wondering what you'd think of calling it The Good Shepherd Veterinary Clinic? After everything you and Vasi have been through, it got me thinking about our veterinary profession. It's not just about healing animals, about what we can do for them. They give us back so much more. Especially our shepherd dogs. They work for us without question, they love us without conditions, they are loyal, they don't judge us, they don't hold grudges." She paused, her hands resting on Vasi's back. "So, what do you think, Rika?" she whispered.

"The Good Shepherd. Yeah, that would work. What do you think, Vasi, huh?" Rika wrapped her arms around Vasi's neck and buried her head in his thick coat so they would not see her fresh tears. Tears of relief, joy, sorrow, gratitude. Tears of second chances. She was one lucky girl.

Acknowledgements

There are many people who have enriched my life through our connections with dogs, and Akbash Dogs in particular. I am especially grateful to those who have taught me so much about dogs and livestock. For the many hours of conversations by phone, letter, email, and in person, I thank Marsha Peterson and Diane Spisak. For their dedication to the conservation of this amazing breed, I also thank Anita Dobrzelecki, Martine Dubuc, Rene Fleming, Hazel Plumbley, Ilker Unlu and David Sims.

I also wish to acknowledge a wise and youthful reader, Emma Chilton, for her thoughtful comments, and the considerate, sensitive work of my editors, Penelope Jackson and Laurie Brinklow. Their input was much appreciated. I am also grateful to my Dutch consultants, Cathy Schaap and Geesje Nienhuis. And, as always, my deepest gratitude and love to my group of talented, big-hearted sister-writers, and the generous support of the awesome writing and arts community of Prince Edward Island.

My heartfelt thanks to all the people who have cared for and loved these beautiful, hard-working dogs. We can learn much from our canine companions and helpmates—patience, empathy, and kindness, for instance—and share those qualities with the other humans and animals on our planet.